John R. Illingwoth

Divine Immanence

John R. Illingwoth

Divine Immanence

ISBN/EAN: 9783743367111

Manufactured in Europe, USA, Canada, Australia, Japa

Cover: Foto ©Andreas Hilbeck / pixelio.de

Manufactured and distributed by brebook publishing software (www.brebook.com)

John R. Illingwoth

Divine Immanence

DIVINE IMMANENCE

AN ESSAY

ON

THE SPIRITUAL SIGNIFICANCE OF MATTER

BY

J. R. ILLINGWORTH, M.A.

AUTHOR OF 'PERSONALITY HUMAN AND DIVINE'

Οἶον γὰρ ἕκαστόν ἐστι τῆς γενέσεως τελεσθείσης, ταύτην φαμὲν τὴν φύσιν εἶναι ἑκάστου.—ARIST. *Pol.*

London

MACMILLAN AND CO., LIMITED

NEW YORK: THE MACMILLAN COMPANY

1898

Oxford

HORACE HART, PRINTER TO THE UNIVERSITY

PREFACE

MUCH of the best philosophical writing in England, of late years, has been critical, or, in the technical and proper sense of the word, sceptical. But critical and sceptical phases, in the progress of thought, can never, from their very nature, be other than temporary things : they sift and question the constructions of the past ; but only with a view to prepare for those that are to come. For the world, after all, is a fact ; sun, moon, and stars are real ; men and women live and love ; the moral law is strong ;—in a word, the universe exists, and some positive account of it must needs be true ; it can never be finally explained by a negation. Hence the result of recent criticism has been to make the need of reconstruction more apparent ; and men are consequently feeling, in various directions, after positive, synthetic ways of thought.

The following brief essay is not an attempt to make any new or original contribution toward such thought : but it is written in the interest of synthesis, and aims at combining some ideas, which are familiar enough in themselves, but are not always viewed in combination—ideas on the relation of nature to religion. For one love, amid all our discord, unites the modern world; we all of us love nature in our several ways; men of science, poets, painters, men of religion, men of affairs, are equally affected by its spell—the wonder of its processes, the glory of its aspect, the contrast of its calmness to the coil of human care. And with this feeling for nature—which, we are probably right in supposing, was never so widely diffused as at the present day—comes an increased susceptibility to those spiritual emotions which the presence of nature inspires, and which lie at the root of what we call natural religion. The sense of natural religion is therefore strong in the modern mind; and this of itself is an important step towards positive, constructive belief. But we, of later ages, for whom history has happened, can never again revert to a mere religion of nature; any more than to a state of nature, in society, or policy, or morals. For we have learned, from nature itself, that the law of life is evolution, and that evolution means an increase of distinctive form. Religion, like all other things, must have become, as in fact it has become, increasingly articulate with the process of the years; its development more definite, or, in religious language, its revelation more precise. And the plea of this essay is that the Incarnation is the congruous climax of such development; that the more we analyse natural religion, the more it tends to such an issue; while conversely the Incarnation presupposes such a past. This is no more, of course, than theologians, in all ages, have maintained; and to many readers, therefore, it may seem a commonplace. But its restatement will, perhaps, be permitted for the benefit of those who are more attracted by the question than acquainted with its history; in the hope that some who, under modern influence, have felt the fascination of natural religion, may be led to recognize its culmination in the Christian creed.

As this essay is in some sense a sequel to my lectures on 'Personality'—being a further application of the same line of thought—I have here assumed certain positions, which are there defended at length; and at the same time enlarged upon certain others—more especially in the Appendix—which seemed, in their present connexion, to need further emphasis.

CONTENTS

CHAPTER I.

MATTER AND SPIRIT.

CHAPTER III.

DIVINE IMMANENCE IN NATURE.

CHAPTER IV.

DIVINE IMMANENCE IN MAN.

CHAPTER V.

THE INCARNATION AND MIRACLES.

CHAPTER VI.

THE INCARNATION AND SACRAMENTS.

CHAPTER VII.

THE INCARNATION AND THE TRINITY.

APPENDIX.

DIVINE IMMANENCE

CHAPTER I

MATTER AND SPIRIT

THE nature of the relation between spirit
and matter may perhaps be thought too ab-
struse a problem to be of general interest. Yet
it is a question which lies at the root of all our
different theories of life; of our art, of our moral
conduct, of our religion or irreligion; of the gloom
that darkens, or the hope that glorifies the sunset
of our days. We all have opinions of one kind or
another on the point, and it deeply concerns us,
seeing the nature of the issues they involve, that
those opinions should, if possible, be true.

The subject is not therefore really unpractical,
or remote from common interest; and, as it has
been much discussed of recent years, for various
reasons, and from various points of view, no
apology will perhaps be needed, for one more
recurrence to the question, in its bearing on religious life and thought.

B

Body and soul is a distinction which dates from primitive philosophy; we find it, in crude conception, among the earliest and rudest races; whether drawn from the visions of dreamland or elsewhere. And with the progress of reflection this distinction gradually passed, after much sifting and refinement by successive schools of thought, into the more complete and comprehensive antithesis, between what we now call spirit and matter.

Now the first thing to notice about spirit and matter is that, however we regard them,—whether as totally different things, or as different aspects of the same thing,—we only know them as a fact in combination.

First, there is the material world outside us, earth, sea, sky, and sun, and stars; the manifold movement of its processes, the life with which it teems, the beauty of its aspect, the music of its sounds. It existed before we were born—this solid universe of things—and will continue to exist when we are gone. We cannot easily be brought to regard it as in any way dependent upon ourselves, and we are always ready to 'vanquish Berkeley with a grin.' Yet a little reflection will convince us that our knowledge of the world is largely qualified and coloured by the constitution of our mind. The mind receives its information, to begin with, from the senses, and the impressions of sense are very different from the things which

they reflect. The hues of the sunset and the rain-
bow, with all their power to move the soul, are
due to movements among atoms to which we can
ascribe no colour; and the musical sounds that
seem to us so spiritual, flow from vibrations—
merely mechanical vibrations—of the air. The
same is the case with the other senses; they only
present us with effects. While scientific men assure
us that even sensitive perception is by no means so
simple a process as it seems, and involves acts of
combination, and comparison, and inference which,
however instinctively performed, are in their nature
intellectual. And when we pass from simple to
complex perceptions, this action of the mind becomes quite obvious. In looking at a landscape,
for instance, we see more than a parti-coloured
panorama, which is, of course, all that is reflected
in the eye; we distinguish and recognize its features,
trees, flowers, houses, cattle, birds; and this implies previous knowledge, and memory, and thought;
we interpret what we see, and though custom has
made the process automatic, it is none the less of
mental origin. The primary aspect of the world
therefore does not show us matter by itself, but
matter as it affects our mind, in a particular way,
through the senses, and is at the same moment
affected in particular ways by our mind. Nor does
science alter the case. Science indeed penetrates
behind this primary aspect of the world, and

presents us with a different picture. It discovers
the machinery by which the scenic effect is produced; atoms, energy, ether, and the laws which
they obey, or in other words, the ways in which
they act. But all this brings us no nearer to the
knowledge of matter by itself. On the contrary,
it lands us in a region of theories, hypotheses, ideas,
which, however true we may believe them to be,
are not material but mental. Thus matter, as we
know it, is everywhere and always fused with
mind: and in the nature of the case it always
must be so; for 'to know a thing,' of course, means
to bring it into relation to our mind; and our
mind, as we have seen, is not a mirror which
passively reflects, but an agent which helps to
constitute the object of its ken.

The case is the same when we turn to spirit, for
that also, as we know it, is always connected with
matter. Not only do we depend on the senses,
which are material things, to awaken our intelligence, and feeling, and will; but we cannot think
at all, we cannot be conscious, without a brain,
changes in which accompany our every change of
thought.

The fact, indeed, that we are unaware of the
movements taking place in our brain, may sometimes mislead us into speaking of purely spiritual
experience; but no experience, however spiritual,
can be other than a state of consciousness, and

therefore of the material organ upon which consciousness depends.

But if matter and spirit are thus only known in
combination, it follows that neither can be completely known; since we cannot disentangle their
respective contributions to the joint result which we
call 'experience.' Hence it is that every possible
shade of opinion has existed on the relationship
between the two; from the view that regards
mind as a passing harmony of matter, to the view
that regards matter as a dream of mind. What
we actually know, at first hand, is our personal
experience, in which the two factors are inex-
tricably combined; and directly we go beyond this
to speak of matter or spirit by themselves, we are
making abstraction of one element from our concrete experience, without any means of knowing
whether such an abstraction can exist, except in
the mind that makes it. It is, of course, logically
possible that the two things may be independent
and separable realities, as the natural dualists or
natural realists believe; or that either may be a
mere mode of the other, as idealism and materialism respectively maintain; or yet again, that the
two may be co-ordinate aspects, or manifestations,
or functions of one reality. The claims of this
latter opinion have been revived of recent years
under the name of monism; but it should be
remembered that monism is not really newer than

any of the alternative conjectures; they are all as old as philosophy, and remain conjectures still.

But leaving conjecture for the present, and limiting our thoughts to what we know, we find that though we cannot in fact separate spirit and matter, yet the two words represent very distinct phases of our total experience; and phases which, whatever the nature of their ultimate connexion, are perfectly separable in thought. Thus the fundamental characteristic of spirit, as we know it in human personality, is self-consciousness, the power to make mental distinction between self and other things, and to regard all other things as objects over against our subjective self: while spiritual life consists in the free selection, and conscious pursuit of the various objects of knowledge, affection, or practical endeavour, which we are thus able to present to ourselves. Our action is thus determined, in technical terms, by final causes; that is, by causes which do not exercise a physical compulsion, but appeal to the mind as ends, aims, purposes, ideals, which we are free either to follow or refuse. Hence we are self-determined; since, from the objects that occur to us, we can choose the one which we shall make our own; and as by successive acts of choice we gradually mould and shape our character, we are, in a measure, self-creative, causes of ourselves (*caussae sui*). This capacity of self-determination, and therefore of self-creation, compels us to place spirit in a rank by itself. Other things are determined from without; they are what external forces make them; they do not choose what they will be. But spirit chooses its own end, elects what it will become, and thereby asserts its existence, as having a value for itself. And a being which thus claims to exist for its own sake, and be its own end, thereby justifies its existence : it has in our eyes a right to exist, by the very fact of willing its own existence. It has, as we say, an absolute value compared with merely material things, whose reason for existence lies in their relation to other things outside themselves; like cogs in a wheel, links in a chain, fragments of a machine or picture that possess no meaning when detached from the whole.

Regarded simply from a metaphysical point of view then, as self-conscious and self-determined, spirit reigns in a realm apart. But of course it is much more than a metaphysical abstraction; it is ethical and emotional as well. Its power of self-determination enables it to act from a sense of duty, to obey a moral law, and in so doing become good; while its goodness finds highest expression in the life of self-sacrificing love, which is only possible to a being that is both self-conscious and free; and which we recognize as the end of ends, the reality that needs no explanation.

'For life, with all it yields, of joy and woe
   And hope and fear,—believe the aged friend,—
   Is just our chance of the prize of learning love,
   How love might be, hath been indeed, and is[1].'

Then as to matter: what do we know of it? The term is often used as if it implied some common stuff, of which individual things are made. But no analysis has yet been able to detect such a common stuff. On the contrary, we find a number of primitive elements, which recent science, instead of diminishing has considerably increased. Matter is the sum total of all these elements, regarded as possessing a particular attribute, namely materiality, or the property of occupying space: while, as all the occupants of space are in motion, molecular or molar, occupation of space may be said to be practically synonymous with movement in space. Matter then is the name for what moves in space. It is at present believed to consist of atoms which have different chemical characteristics, that may possibly be due to different mechanical arrangements; but here we pass into the region of hypothesis, and beyond this all is hypothetical as to what atoms ultimately are. At any rate, their ultimate constitution is out of reach of our senses; and it remains that matter as we know it is an effect, a phenomenon or appearance, a manifestation of something other than meets either hand or eye.

[1] Browning, *A Death in the Desert.*

Briefly then spirit is what thinks and wills and loves; and matter is what moves in space: and whatever their ultimate relationship may be, we may fairly speak of two things whose modes of manifestation are so different, as for practical purposes two different things. Adopting this use of language then, the next fact which we wish to note is that, while matter is of use to spirit, spirit is of no use to matter.

One might, of course, put the case in a more general form, by substituting 'consciousness' for 'spirit,' and saying that, while matter is of use to consciousness, consciousness is of no use to matter; thus including in the statement every form of conscious life, from the lowest sensitive organism upward. But what is true, in its measure, of all conscious life, is true in a much more eminent degree of spirit. And, as spirit is the thing with which we are dealing, we will confine our attention to that; merely remarking that the same line of thought admits of this wider application.

While then matter is of use—incessant and inevitable use—to spirit, spirit, on the other hand, is of no use to matter. Man can improve material things, of course, from his own point of view, by employing them for purposes of science or of art; but in so doing, he only alters their relation to himself; he does not and cannot change their nature. Electricity gains nothing by guidance along wires; marble remains marble, as much in the statue as in the rock; gold is no better for coinage, nor flowers for cultivation, except in their relationship to man. Human interference does not anywise affect, either the constitution of natural elements, or the action of natural laws.

But reverse the picture, and the opposite is the case. Our every state of consciousness depends, as we have seen, upon the brain, and therefore upon the blood that nourishes the brain, and therefore on the chemical elements that form the blood. Without oxygen, and nitrogen, and phosphorus, and carbon, we could neither think, nor will, nor love.

But thought and will and love must needs communicate themselves to others; spirit craves intercourse with spirit; and here again we depend on matter. Tongue and ear are material things; words are movements of the air; and printing press and telegraph extend their sway. Machinery again, with its coal, and steam, and iron, is ever at work to enlarge the practical dominion of our will; while art—art takes up the stubborn elements of earth and transmutes them in its crucible to spiritual things. Hellenic sculptures, Gothic cathedrals, mediaeval painting, modern music, are only modes of matter, when regarded by themselves: yet through them the soul of man has given utterance and permanence to all the varying phases of his inward spiritual story; which else would have been fugitive and dumb.

Further, to give expression to a thing is to realize it, in the sense of making it more real; and hence matter, as being the language of spirit, is also the medium of its realization. Thoughts float idly across the mind, till they have been precipitated in print; theories remain abstract and uncertain, till they have been tested by experiment; good intentions are of no avail, till they have faced the resistance of the outer world, and in overcoming its opposition become moral acts; and love can never rest, till it has proved its own intensity by a thousand tender, thoughtful, self-sacrificing deeds. In every case contact with matter strengthens the spiritual fibre, forcing vagueness into outline, confusion into clearness, doubt into decision, hesitation into act. It is the necessary means by which our spiritual life becomes actual, concrete, real. Nor is it only as a means of expression that matter ministers to spirit. It has also an important reaction upon character and conduct.

'The floating clouds their state shall lend
To her; for her the willow bend;
Nor shall she fail to see
Even in the motions of the storm
Grace that shall mould the maiden's form
By silent sympathy.

'The stars of midnight shall be dear
To her; and she shall lean her ear
In many a secret place
Where rivulets dance their wayward round,
And beauty born of murmuring sound
Shall pass into her face[1].'

This is more than a poet's conceit. It is a description of what happens daily, and in more ways than most men are aware; the gradual moulding of our thoughts and feelings, our habitual expression, our face and form, by subtle influence of outward things. Plato first called attention to this principle, and it has been called from him, platonic. But all great thinkers have recognized its action, from Plato to the present day. None more so than Browning. Has a man reasoned himself into unbelief? Then—

'Just when we're safest
There's a sunset touch, a fancy from
A flower bell[2],'

and the reasoning fades away. Have the souls of two lovers been melted into one?

'The forests had done it; there they stood;
We caught for a moment the powers at play:
They had mingled us so for once and good,
Their work was done[3].'

---

[1] Wordsworth, 'Three years she grew.'
[2] Browning, *Bishop Blougram's Apology*.
[3] Id. *By the Fireside.*

Have two others missed their mutual vocation?
They have profaned in so doing a natural sacrament, which ' made things plain in vain.'

> ' What was the sea for? What, the grey,
>   Sad church, that solitary day,
>   Crosses and graves and swallow's call?
> Was there naught better than to enjoy?
> No feat which, done, would make time break
> And let us pent-up creatures through
> Into eternity, our due?
> No forcing earth teach heaven's employ[1]? '

Nor are such things exceptional; they are
common situations of every day, and must have
recurred, since primaeval man first wove his legends
of the dawn; matter everywhere and always,
fashioning, inspiring, controlling, quickening, the
processes of spiritual life.

Here then we are face to face with a plain fact
of experience. Throughout the entire range of their
co-existent activity, matter subserves spirit, and that
not in one way only, but in a variety of subtle,
and delicate, and complex ways; while in the
opposite direction, nothing of the kind takes place.

When therefore we find that the material world,
which can derive, as we have already seen, no
possible benefit from spirit, is in countless ways
adapted to further spiritual life; it is hard to
resist the conclusion that matter exists for this

[1] Browning, *Dis Aliter Visum.*

very end, and that all its ingenuity of intricate
arrangement is meant to serve the purpose, which
in fact it so elaborately serves. If matter lay at
our feet, as a thing to be employed or neglected
at will, the case would be different; and we might
then regard its use as accidental. But its fusion
with spirit is, in fact, far too intimate, its correlation too exact to admit of any such idea. It is
obviously part and parcel of the same system with
spirit; and if so must, we argue, be qualified throughout by the final causality which is spirit's goal.

'Since, in the seeing soul, all worth lies, I assert,—
And nought i' the world, which, save for soul
    that sees, inert
Was, is, and would be ever,—stuff for trans-
    muting,—null
And void until man's breath evoke the beautiful[1].'

The case may, for the sake of emphasis, be
re-stated thus. We attribute an absolute worth and
dignity to spirit, simply because it possesses the
power of purpose, purposeful thought, purposeful
action, purposeful love. Purpose is our standard,
our inevitable standard of value; not this or that
particular purpose, which may be useful to ourselves, but purpose as such, the free determination
to realize a foreseen end. Our mental constitution
compels us to attribute this importance to the

[1] Browning, *Fifine at the Fair*, 55.

power of purpose; or, to put it otherwise, our reason justifies us in so doing. Now this does not merely mean that we prefer things which have a purpose to things which have none. It means that purpose, when once recognized, becomes the necessary and self-evident key to existence; the final category, or form of thought, under which we are compelled to regard the world. For a system which culminates in purpose must be purposeful throughout. Its entire process must be qualified by the character of its conclusion. And hence the material order which is so marvellously ministrant to spirit must, we conclude, be intended so to be. Spirit must be its final cause.

There is of course a prejudice, in many minds, against all consideration of final causes; which Bacon calls 'anthropomorphic conceptions, rather than cosmic realities' (*ex analogia hominis magis quam universi*), and Spinoza, 'mere figments of the human brain' (*nihil nisi humana figmenta*). But what really provoked this criticism was the frivolous and futile teleology, which substituted the thought of final for that of physical causation; leading men to think they knew enough about a thing, when they knew its presumed purpose—often a very credulously and crudely presumed purpose—and to neglect all further inquiry into its process of production, that is to say, all interest in physical science. But Bacon fully admits, elsewhere, that 'final causes have their place': and as the subject is important and his authority has weight, it may be worth while to quote him at length.

'For to say *that the hairs of the eye-lids are for a quickset and fence about the sight;* or that *the firmness of the skins and hides of living creatures is to defend them from the extremities of heat or cold;* or that *the bones are for the columns or beams, whereupon the frames of the bodies of living creatures are built;* or that *the leaves of trees are for protecting of the fruit;* or that *the clouds are for watering of the earth;* or that *the solidness of the earth is for the station and mansion of living creatures* and the like, is well inquired and collected in metaphysique, but in physique they are impertinent. . . . Not because those final causes are not true, and worthy to be inquired, being kept within their own province; but because their excursions into the limits of physical causes hath bred a vastness and solitude in that track. For otherwise, keeping their precincts and borders, men are extremely deceived if they think there is an enmity or repugnancy at all between them . . . both causes being true and compatible, the one declaring an *intention*, the other a *consequence* only. Neither doth this call in question, or derogate from Divine Providence, but highly confirm and exalt it. For as in civil actions he is the greater and deeper politique, that can make other men the instruments of his will and ends, and yet never acquaint them with his purpose, so as they shall do it and yet not know what they do, than he that imparteth his meaning to those he employeth ; so is the wisdom of God more admirable, when nature intendeth one thing, and Providence draweth forth another, than if He had communicated to particular creatures and motions the characters and impressions of His Providence.'

Spinoza's objection is more thorough-going, but rests upon an impossible separation between man and the universe. For a universe, apart from and in contrast with the mind that knows it, is a mere creature of the imagination, which cannot be construed into thought ; an utterly unthinkable, meaningless abstraction ; while a universe that is known to mind must be known in subjection to the laws of mind, among which is the teleological principle. But Spinoza's imaginative picture, for all its philosophic impossibility, has been widely influential, during the last two centuries ; through the emphasis it has given to the contrast, so congenial to a scientific age, between the grandeur of the material universe, and the insignificance of man. It is important therefore to notice that such a contrast is entirely fallacious, and merely arises from the fact that we see the magnitude of matter, but cannot see the magnitude of mind. To gain a truer view of their relative proportions, we must begin by confining our attention to the earth; as the only field where we know the two in correlation. For the rest of the stellar universe we see only on its material side; and while all analogy leads us to infer that this must have a spiritual counterpart, we know nothing of its existence, nature, or extent; and discussion of the subject is therefore utterly impossible.

When we confine our view to the earth then, it looms large, when compared with its inhabitants, and endures while their successive generations pass away. But if intensity, rather than extension, be, as we cannot help believing, the true measure and criterion of worth, a single human spirit far out-soars material things. What then of the millions upon millions now inhabiting the earth? and what of all the generations that have passed away, or are to come? Surely, in mere number, and much more when measured by their souls' immensity, they form an aggregate which dwarfs to nothing-ness the size of their temporary home; while if, after all, they should prove immortal, the relative permanence of earthly things will be an illusion— a mere optical illusion.

We will return therefore, without further apology, to the conclusion that we had reached, the conclusion that matter exists for the sake of spirit. Some such assumption, indeed, has always been implicitly present in the popular mind; but our contention is that this assumption, like many another of the implicit convictions of common sense, has a strong metaphysical foundation, in the necessities of human thought; though for the sake of those who are either sceptical or shy of metaphysic, it will suffice to say that it has at least serious probability in its favour.

The statement that matter exists for the sake of spirit, is, it will be noticed, a general formula. It does not imply either that we can trace the utility of every material phenomenon, or that we need suppose every material phenomenon to be subservient to human use: it merely asserts that, within the field of our experience, there is a constant order of relation between the two, which is never reversed; and which justifies the judgement in point. But as we finite beings who use matter, and find it so adapted to our use, have no share in its original production, or control of its general course; we infer that it must be guided by a spiritual Being, of commensurate capacity and will; while further light must of necessity be thrown upon the character of this Being, by the nature of the spiritual purpose which He enables matter to subserve.

This is not, it should be noticed, the form of

teleology, or argument from design, which relies upon detailed cases of adaptation within the material region, and which has been attacked of late years on the ground that the adaptations in question may be only the survivals of many failures. The attack indeed has been adequately answered, but with that we are not now concerned. What we are here contending is that the entire material order, with all its infinite complexity, ministers to another and a higher order of being, from which it receives no reciprocal return, and is therefore intended or designed so to do; and it is in the width and variety of these ministrations that the strength of the argument consists. This may be called the higher teleology; and while it immensely strengthens the probability of design within the material order itself, is unaffected by objections from the material side. It can only be met, as we have seen, by denying the veracity of our faculties. Man, from the dawn of history, has asked why? as well as how? why am I? and why is the world? as well as how came it all to be? And as long as he refuses to be satisfied without an answer to that Why? he remains an unconscious metaphysician, a believer in final causation. When we are complacently told in certain quarters that the Copernican astronomy revolutionized man's view of his relation to the universe, we should remember that to say the least, this is a considerable overstatement of the case. In minds of a materialistic bias, it would undoubtedly have this effect; but not in those who estimated man by the claims of his spiritual nature, which is as unaffected by the size of his dwelling-place as by the cubits of his stature. And what Copernicus did for space, modern science has done for time. It has dwarfed the spiritual history of man by comparison with the infinitude of ages, during which the material system that he inhabits was evolved. But still it is true that spirit thinks, and wills, and loves, while matter only moves in space ; and man's judgement of their relative importance, therefore, remains what it was before.

In conclusion, it should be noticed that if there is truth in the foregoing remarks, it is absolutely unaffected by any theory which we may adopt, as to the ultimate nature of matter ; for it deals with the relations between matter and spirit as we know them ; and is as compatible with the most realistic conceptions of matter, as with those more sub-limated views of it, to which some modern thinkers seem disposed to return.

CHAPTER II

AMONG the various uses of matter to spirit, which we have mentioned in the preceding chapter, one of the most striking throughout all history has been its religious use ; the part which it has played by its mere aspect, or by obvious inference from its aspect, in awakening and sustaining religious ideas.

Sun-myths, star-myths, storm-myths, myths of the mountains, and the rivers, and the trees, lie at the root, as we now know so well, of all early religion. And when with the progress of reflection these myths were criticized and sifted, man still found in the grandeur, the harmony, the beauty, the marvellous mechanism, the exuberant life, the exquisite adaptations of the natural world, evidence of the existence and character of God ; evidence which, whatever may be urged against its value, has, as a simple fact of history, weighed with man in every age. Nor has all our modern enlightenment materially altered our case. We have long outgrown mythology, and are intolerant of doubtful logic ; but the religious influence of external nature is as strong upon us as it ever was, possibly even stronger than in some bygone times. For the strength of the influence in question is emotional rather than intellectual, and consists in a sense of nearness or communion, of one kind or another, with the divine. And though this admits of intellectual analysis, and can be fashioned into argument, it is the sense of experience in the background which gives the argument its force.

Now this is a fact of greater significance than is commonly supposed ; and to estimate it duly we must endeavour to form a mental picture of the scale on which the influence in question has obtained. Though, therefore, it may almost seem like offering a brick, as an adequate specimen of a house, we will quote a few passages bearing on the subject : the point to notice in them being the fact that in all ages of the world, and under every variety of culture, and of creed, nature—material nature—the course and aspect of the outer world has been an influence, and a main influence, making for religion.

To begin with what Egyptologists assure us is the oldest poem in the world ; the 15th chapter of the Book of the Dead contains a hymn to the rising and setting sun :—

' Hail to thee, Ra, the self-existent. . . . Glorious is thine uprising from the horizon. Both worlds

are illumined by thy rays. All the gods rejoice
to see the king of heaven . . . all men rejoice to see
thee marching in thy mystery towards them . . .
thee who art given anew to them every morning . . .
thy splendour is beyond compare . . . it has all the
colours of Arabia. . . . Hail to thee who makest
glad the lands, and all their towns and temples with
the blessings of thy goodness . . . thou who bringest
forth food and sweet nourishment. . . . Hail to thee,
Ra, when thou returnest home in renewed beauty,
crowned, and almighty[1].'

The same thoughts are expanded in a later hymn,
which is still not later than the age of Moses :—

'Praise to Amen-Ra :

     .   .   .   .

the good god beloved :
giving life to all animated things :
to all fair cattle :

     .   .   .   .

Maker of men, Creator of beasts :
Lord of existences, Creator of fruitful trees :
Maker of herbs, Feeder of cattle :

     .   .   .   .

Maker of things below and above, Enlightener of
     the earth :
sailing in heaven in tranquillity :

     .   .   .   .

at whose pleasure the Nile overflows :

[1] Trans. from French of Lefébure.

Lord of mercy most loving:
at whose coming men live:
opener of every eye:
proceeding from the firmament:
causer of pleasure and light.

.   .   .   .

thy love pervades the earth:

.   .   .   .

maker of grass for the cattle:
fruitful trees for men:
causing the fish to live in the river:
the birds to fill the air:
giving breath to those in the egg:
feeding the bird that flies:
giving food to the bird that perches:
to the creeping thing and the flying thing equally:
providing food for the rats in their holes:
feeding the flying *things* in every tree.
Hail to thee for all these things:

.   .   .   .

homage to thee in all their voices:

.   .   .   .

Hail to thee say all creatures:
salutation to thee from every land:
to the height of heaven, to the breadth of the
    earth:
to the depths of the sea:
the gods adore thy Majesty:
the spirits thou hast created exalt (thee):

rejoicing before the feet of their begetter :
they cry out welcome to thee :
father of the fathers of all gods :
who raises the heavens who fixes the earth [1].'

It is a far cry from Egypt to the plains of India, both in distance and in race : yet in the Vedas, the earliest literature of our Indo-European kindred, a similar note is struck. Their theology is for the most part polytheistic, passing at times into pantheism ; but the spectacle of nature in its varying aspects of power, beauty, and beneficence, is the dominating motive of it all :—

'May the Earth and the Heaven hear us, the Water, the Sun with the stars, the wide Atmosphere.'

'May Mitra, Varuna, Aditi, Ocean, Earth, and Heaven gladden us.'

'May Aditi, the mother of Mitra and the opulent Varuna, preserve us from every calamity.'

'Aditi is the sky ; Aditi is the air ; . . . Aditi is all the gods.'

'Neither heavens nor atmospheres nor earths have equalled Indra the thunderer in might. By Indra the lights of the sky have been fixed and established. Those which are established he has not removed.'

'He has settled the ancient mountains by his might ; he has directed downwards the action of the waters. He has supported the earth, the uni-

[1] *Records of the Past*, ii. 129.

versal nurse. By his skill he has propped up the
sky from falling.'

'Dawn on us with prosperity, O Ushas, daugh-
ter of the sky. . . . O luminous and bountiful
goddess. Ushas advances . . . arousing footed
creatures, and makes the birds fly aloft. The
flying birds no longer rest after thy dawning,
O bringer of food. In thee, when thou dawnest,
O lively goddess, is the life and breath of all creatures. Ushas, like a dancer, puts on her gay attire,
. . . like a fair girl adorned by her mother, . . . like
one rising out of the water in which she has been
bathing. Ushas dawning restores consciousness ;
fair in her aspect she has awakened all creatures to
cheerfulness.'

'Mother of the gods, manifestation of Aditi, fore-
runner of the sacrifice, mighty Ushas, shine forth !
Arise, bestowing approbation on our prayer. . . .
May Mitra, Varuna, Aditi, the Ocean, the Earth,
and the Sky, bestow upon us those brilliant and
excellent resources which the Dawns bring to the
man who offers sacrifice and praise.'

'Thou createst light, O Sūrya, and illuminatest
the whole firmament. . . . Thou, O Sūrya, pene-
tratest the sky, the broad firmament, measuring out
the days with thy rays, spying out all creatures.
Seven ruddy mares bear thee onward in thy chariot,
O clear-sighted Sūrya, the god with flaming locks.'

'Come hither, Maruts (storm-gods) on your

chariots charged with lightning. ... Harness the red mares to the chariots, harness the ruddy horses to the chariots.... I call hither this your host, brilliant on chariots, terrible and glorious. ... Through fear of you, ye terrible ones, the forests even bend down, the earth shakes, and also the mountain (cloud). May your water-carriers come here to-day, all the Maruts who stir up the rain.... When you have come forth, O Maruts, the waters gush, the forests go asunder [1].'

'Now for the greatness of the chariot of Vâta! Its roar goes crashing and thundering. It moves touching the sky, and creating red sheens, or it goes scattering the dust of the earth. ...

'When he moves on his paths along the sky, he rests not even a single day ; the friend of the waters, the first-born, the holy, where was he born, whence did he spring?

'The breath of the gods, the germ of the world, that god moves wherever he listeth ; his roars indeed are heard, not his form—let us offer sacrifice to that Vâta [2]!'

When we turn to the kindred, but far more ethical, religion of the Avesta, the distinction between creator and creature is more clearly drawn; but the recognition of the former, in and by means of the latter, is none the less apparent :—

[1] Muir's *Sanskrit Texts*, vol. v.
[2] *Sacred Books of the East*, xxxii. 449.

' I desire to approach Ahura and Mithra with my praise, the lofty, eternal, and the holy two ; and I desire to approach the stars, moon, and sun . . . with my praise . . . and I desire to approach all the mountains with my praise, glorious with sanctity as they are, and with abundant glory.

' And I offer . . . to Ahura and Mithra, . . . the holy two, and to the stars which are the creatures of Spe*n*ta Mainyu, . . . and to the Moon which contains the seed of cattle in its beams, and to the resplendent Sun of the fleet horses . . . and to these places, districts, pastures, and abodes with their springs of water, and to the waters and the lands, and the plants, and to this earth and yon heaven, and to the holy wind, and to the stars, and the moon, even to the stars without beginning (to their course), the self-appointed, and to all the holy creatures of Spe*n*ta Mainyu.

' We worship thee, the Fire, O Ahura Mazda's son . . . and we worship the good and best waters Mazda-made, holy, all the waters Mazda-made and holy, and all the plants which Mazda made, and which are holy.

' Thus do we worship Ahura Mazda, who made the Kine . . . and the waters, and the wholesome plants, the stars, and the earth, and all . . . objects that are good. Yea, we worship Him for His Sovereign Power and His greatness, beneficent . . . and we worship this earth that bears us, together with

Thy wives, O Ahura Mazda ! . . . O ye waters ! now we worship you, you that are showered down, and you that stand in pools and vats, . . . ye female Ahuras of Ahura, you that serve us in helpful ways, well forded and full-flowing, and effective for the bathings.

'And we sacrifice to the fountains of the waters, and to the fordings of the rivers, to the forkings of the highways, and to the meetings of the roads.

'And we sacrifice to the hills that run with torrents, and the lakes that brim with waters, and to the corn that fills the corn-fields ; and we sacrifice to both the protector and the Creator, to both Zarathustra and the Lord.

'And we sacrifice to both earth and heaven, and to the stormy wind that Mazda made, and to the peak of high Haraiti, and to the land, and all things good [1].'

Passing from Persia to Palestine, we enter a still purer religious atmosphere ; but the clear monotheism and high morality of the later Hebrews only enhance the prominence of nature in their devotional literature :—

'The heavens declare the glory of God, and the firmament sheweth His handiwork.'

'He telleth the number of the stars, and calleth them all by their names.'

[1] *Sacred Books of the East*, xxxi.

'The sea is His, and He made it, and His hands prepared the dry land.'

'Who in His strength setteth fast the mountains, and is girded about with power.'

'He gathereth the waters of the sea together as it were upon an heap, and layeth up the deep as in a treasure house.'

'He bringeth forth the clouds from the ends of the world; and sendeth forth lightnings with the rain, bringing the winds out of His treasuries.'

'It is the Lord that commandeth the waters; it is the glorious God that maketh the thunder. It is the Lord that ruleth the sea, the voice of the Lord is mighty in operation, the voice of the Lord is a glorious voice.'

'He rode upon the cherubims and did fly: He came flying upon the wings of the wind.'

'He made darkness His secret place; His pavilion round about Him with dark waters and thick clouds to cover Him.'

'He giveth snow like wool, and scattereth the hoar-frost like ashes; He casteth forth His ice like morsels; who is able to abide His frost? He sendeth out His word and melteth them, He bloweth with His wind, and the waters flow.'

'Praise Him, sun and moon, praise Him, all ye stars and light. . . . Fire and hail, snow and vapours, wind and storm, fulfilling His word; mountains and all hills; fruitful trees and all cedars, beasts and all cattle; worms and feathered fowls.'

'Thou deckest Thyself with light as it were with a garment, and spreadest out the heavens like a curtain.'

'Thy way is in the sea, and Thy paths in the great waters, and Thy footsteps are not known.'

'Thou that makest the outgoings of the morning and evening to praise Thee[1].'

Passing on from Hebrew to Greek and Roman literature, we return to pantheistic and polytheistic modes of thought, but the influence of nature is evident in both.

'Zeus is the air, and Zeus the earth and heaven,
    And all things; and what else is over all[2],'

says Aeschylus.

'Men have inferred,' says Virgil, 'from the instincts of the bees, that they partake of the divine mind, and breath of heaven:'—

'for God pervades the whole
Earth and the spacious sea, and heaven profound[3].'

And again—

'An inward spirit feeds earth, heaven, and sea,
    The shining moon, and giant stars; a mind
    Pervades their limbs, and moves the mighty
        mass[4].'

[1] The Psalms.   [2] Clem. Alex. *Strom.* v.
[3] Virgil, *Georg.* iv. 220.   [4] Id. *Aeneid*, vi. 724.

And Lucan, again—

'Whate'er thou seest, where'er thou goest is Jove.'

Such pantheistic passages might easily be multiplied, while those of a more polytheistic tone are too numerous to admit of selection. A single typical instance must suffice — the famous apostrophe of Prometheus :—

'O holy heaven, and ye winged winds
  And springs of waters, and unnumbered smiles
  Of ocean waves; and thee all-mother earth,
  And thee all-seeing circle of the sun, I call
  To witness what I suffer [1].'

In an artificial age such language might be called merely poetical, in the sense of meaningless ; but there is no question that for the Greek it was full of serious reality.

But after all, as Bacon remarks, '*Ethnicis moralis philosophia vice theologiae erat,*'—the moral philosophers were the religious teachers of pagan antiquity.

And though it is difficult, of course, to generalize on so wide a subject as Greek philosophy, one may safely go so far as to say that in all its forms and stages, with the exception of one somewhat subordinate school, it was characterized by the recognition of reason in nature. The early thinkers with their pregnant sayings—'All things are full of

[1] Aesch. *Prom. Vinct.* 88.

D

gods'—'All was chaos till mind arranged it'—
'Thought and being are one'; Socrates, Plato, and
Aristotle, with their insistence on rational causation; the Stoics and Neo-platonists, with their
diverse forms of pantheism, were alike influenced
by the picture of the material world, its order and
its harmony, its beauty and its use, as suggestive
of divine guidance, either from above or from
within.   Plato viewed the world, and especially its
beauty, as the manifestation of divine ideas that
were more real than itself; Aristotle tended to
view it as the realization of divine ideas, that
without material embodiment would have been
abstract and incomplete.   The one doctrine led
to the transcendent God of the Neo-platonists, the
other to the immanent God of the Stoics; but for
both schools alike, though in different ways, matter
was religiously significant.

'The thoughtful contemplation of nature,' says
Cicero, 'is food to our minds.   We are ennobled
and uplifted above human affairs, and learn to look
down on our own littleness, by thinking on the
grandeur of the heavens above [1].'

'For what else is nature?' asks Seneca, 'but
God and Divine reason, immanent in the world and
all its parts [2].' ... 'What is God?   The sum total
of all thou seest, and of all thou canst not see [3].'

---

[1] Cic. *De Nat. Deor.* ii. 41.   [2] Sen. *Nat. Qu.* ii. 45.
[3] Id. *Prol.* 13.

Christianity, with its correlative doctrines of the Trinity and the Incarnation, laid equal stress both on the transcendence and immanence of God, or in less technical terms upon His supremacy and His omnipresence, and was enabled therefore to appropriate and utilize both Neo-platonic and Stoic thought, but with a tenderer appreciation of nature that is distinctively its own. Origen, the first systematic teacher of theology, is described to us as beginning his instructions with the 'high and holy and most beautiful' study of 'the sacred economy of the universe.' And modern readers, whose notion of the Christian Fathers is often merely of ponderous folios upon dusty shelves, would be surprised at their loving interest in the sights and sounds of the natural world.

'The wider our contemplation of creation,' says St. Cyril, 'the grander is our conception of God[1].'

'Earth,' says St. Basil,—'Earth, air, sky, water, day, night, all things visible, remind us who is our benefactor[2].' 'The more profoundly we penetrate the laws on which the universe is founded and sustained, the more do we behold the glory of the Lord[3].'

And again—

'If ever on a bright night, while gazing at the stars in all their beauty, you have thought of the

[1] Cyril Jerus. *Cat.* ix. 2.   [2] Basil, *Hex.* iii. 10.
[3] Id. *In Ps.* xxxiii.

Creator of all things; if you have asked yourself who it is that has bespangled heaven with such flowers, and endowed all things with usefulness even greater than their beauty; if ever in the day-time you have studied the wonders of the light and raised yourself by things visible to the invisible Being, then you are a fit auditor (of Christian truth)[1].'

Gregory of Nyssa, Basil's brother and fellow-follower of Origen, has similar thoughts :—

'Look only,' he says, 'at an ear of corn, at the budding of a plant, at a bunch of ripe grapes, at the beauty in fruit and flower of the early autumn; at the mountains, their bases green with grass which no human hand has sown, while their summits cleave the azure of the sky; at the springs that issue from their swelling slopes like fruitful breasts, to run in rivers through the glens; at the sea that receives all waters, yet remains within its bounds; its waves, stayed by the shore-side, which they can never pass beyond. Look at these and such-like sights, and can the eye of reason fail to read in them lessons of eternal truth[2]?'

For 'Matter had its origin in the uncreated loveliness, and throughout the whole range of matter there are echoes of spiritual beauty, through

---

[1] Basil, *Hex*. vi. 1.   [2] Greg. Nyss. *De mort. inf.*

which we may be led to their immaterial arche-
types[1].'

Nor is it only the Greek Fathers who say things
like this :—

'Who can look on nature,' asks St. Hilary, 'and
not see God[2]?'

'Every aspect and process of nature,' says
Augustine, 'proclaims its Creator ; with diverse
moods and changes like a variety of tongues[3].'

And again, Gregory the Great :—

'If we look attentively enough at outward,
material things, we are recalled by them to inward,
spiritual things. For the wonders of the visible
creation are the footprints of our Creator ; Himself as yet we cannot see, but we are on the road
that leads to vision, when we admire Him in
the things that He has made. And so we call
created things His footprints, since they are made
by Him and guide us to Himself[4].'

Such sentences might indeed be culled from
almost every patristic writer, and are frequently
echoed even in the austere pages of the schoolmen, while we gain glimpses of the same feeling
on the dainty pages of illuminated books, in the
choice of sites for monastic houses and hermits'
homes of prayer, in the countless legends of tender

[1] Dion. Areop. *Cel. Hier.* c. ii.   [2] Hilary, *In Ps.* lii.
[3] Aug. *Lib. Arb.* iii. 70.   [4] Greg. Mag. *Moral.* xxvi. c. xii.

sympathy between the animals and holy men.
The Celtic saints in especial are full of the poetry
of nature, but perhaps its best expression is in the
famous hymn of St. Francis of Assisi :—

' Praised be my Lord God with all His creatures,
and specially our brother the sun, who brings us
the day, and who brings us the light ; fair is he
and shines with a very great splendour : O Lord,
he signifies to us Thee !

' Praised be my Lord for our sister the moon,
and for the stars, the which He has set clear and
lovely in heaven.

' Praised be my Lord for our brother the wind,
and for air and cloud, calms and all weather by
the which Thou upholdest life in all creatures.

' Praised be my Lord for our sister water, who is
very serviceable unto us, and humble and precious
and clean.

' Praised be my Lord for our brother fire, through
whom Thou givest us light in the darkness ; and he
is bright and pleasant and very mighty and strong.

' Praised be my Lord for our mother the earth,
the which doth sustain us and keep us, and bringeth
forth divers fruits and flowers of many colours, and
grass [1].'

When we pass to the Renaissance and the
Reformation with their multitude of writers, selec-

[1] Qu. fr. Sabatier, *Life of St. Francis*, p. 306.

tive quotation from the mass of material becomes almost impossible. Men returned to the study of nature at first hand in every department of life, philosophers, poets, preachers, artists, all alike ; and though of course the effect on some was renewed materialism, countless others recognized the spirituality of matter. This was the case, for instance, with many of the Italian natural philosophers, the men who practically inaugurated that renewed study of nature of which Bacon was content to talk. The poetical pantheism of Giordano Bruno is well known ; but here is a more theistic expression of kindred thoughts from his contemporary Campanella, who was much impressed by the discovery of magnetic attraction, and himself the first to recognize the sexes in plants :—

' All things,' he says, ' feel, or the world would be a chaos. For fire would not aspire, nor stones gravitate, nor waters seek the sea, unless they knew that their continuance depended on leaving their opposite to find their like. . . . For God who is the first power, first wisdom, and first love, has bestowed upon all things the power of existence, and with it such wisdom and such love as shall suffice to continue their existence, for the time that His ruling providence wills them to be. . . . God said, let all things feel, some more some less, as they have more or less necessity to imitate My being ; and let them love to live in that element which they know to be good for them, lest My creation come to naught. Sky and stars are endowed with keenest sensibility ; and we may well suppose that they express their mutual thoughts to one another by the interchange of light, and that their sensibility is full of pleasure [1].'

Mere fantastic poetry this may seem to some, but it has modern affinities among philosophers as well as poets.

Then in literature we find Petrarch, who is the first to show the modern sense of scenery, and whose letters are full of the love of it, speaking of the spiritual thoughts which it inspires :—

'This little spot under the rocks, in the midst of the waters, is more suited than any other to inspire profound thoughts by which the most idle minds may feel themselves lifted to lofty con-templation. . . . How often has night found me still wandering in the fields ! How often have I risen in the silence of a summer night to offer up my prayers and midnight orisons to Christ, and then to steal forth alone . . . to wander by the light of the moon over the fields and mountains [2] !'

While the same note is continually struck by the great painters, who in those delicate backgrounds,

---

[1] Qu. fr. Hallam, *Lit. Eur.* ii. 374.
[2] Trans. in *Century Rev.* liv. 4.

which were the first beginnings of all our modern landscape art, delight to associate the aspects of nature, its smiling pastures, and its storm-rent rocks, with all the varying phases of spiritual life.

Protestant theology stands in sharp contrast with the other movements of the Renaissance. It is the more instructive therefore to notice that in this point they are at one. Here is a passage from the German mystic, Suso :—

' Oh, how cloudlessly and cheerfully the beautiful sun rises in the summer season, and how diligently it gives growth and blessings to the soil; how the leaves and the grass come forth; how the beautiful flowers smile; how the forest, and the heath, and the meadows resound with the sweet songs of the nightingale and other small birds; how all the animals which were shut up during the hard winter come forth and enjoy themselves and go in pairs; how, in humanity, young and old manifest their joy in merry and gladsome utterances! *O tender God! if Thou art so loving in Thy creatures, how fair and lovely must Thou be in Thyself!* Look further, I pray you, and behold the four elements, —earth, water, air, and fire,—and all the wonderful things in them; the variety and diversity of men, beasts, birds, fishes, and the wonders of the deep, all of which cry aloud and proclaim the praise and honour of the boundless and infinite nature of God! O Lord, who preserves all this? Who feeds it? Thou takest care of all, each in its own way, great and small, rich and poor. Thou, God! Thou doest it! Thou, God, art indeed God[1]!'

Luther, again, was notorious for his religious love of nature. But it is not so well known that Zwingli felt the same :—

'From God,' he says, 'as from a fountain, and if I may use the expression, a first material, all things arise into being. By God's power all things exist, live, and operate; even in Him who is everywhere present; and after His pattern who is the essence, the existence, the life of the universe. Nor is man alone of divine origin; but all creatures, though some are nobler and more august than others. Yet all alike are from God and in God, and in proportion to their nobility they express more of the divine power and glory. . . . We recognize in things inanimate, not less than in man, the presence of the divine power by which they exist, and live, and move. God is in the stars; and inasmuch as the stars are from Him and in Him, they have no essence or power or movement of their own; it is all God's, and they are merely the instruments through which the present power of God acts. For for this cause He called creatures into being, that man, from the contemplation of

---

[1] Qu. fr. Hagenbach, *Hist. of Doct. E. T.* ii. 230.

their mutual uses, might learn to recognize God's active presence everywhere, and especially in himself, when he saw it in all things else around [1].'

Catholic theology, again, is fundamentally opposed on many points to Protestant. Yet here they too are agreed. The following passage from Fénélon is thoroughly typical of the great Catholic writers of the seventeenth century. But it might almost be mistaken for a continuation of the above.

'I see God in everything; or rather, I see everything in God. . . . All that exists, exists only by the communication of God's infinite being. All that has intelligence, has it only by derivation from His sovereign reason, and all that acts, acts only from the impulse of His supreme activity. It is He who does all in all; it is He who, at each instant of our life, is the beating of our heart, the movement of our limbs, the light of our eyes, the intelligence of our spirit, the soul of our soul. All that is in us, life, action, thought, will, is the product of His eternal power, and life, and thought, and will [2].'

To these we will add one English voice from the eighteenth century, unlikeliest of times! William Law, who in his later writings was so much influenced by Jacob Boehme,—himself an important

---

[1] Zwingli, *De providentia.*
[2] Fénélon, *Exist. de Dieu*, ii. c. iv; *Necess. de con. Dieu*, n. 18.

link in the tradition we are tracing,—has many passages to the following effect :—

' Look at all nature, through all its height and depth, in all its variety of working powers, it is what it is for this only end, that the hidden riches, the invisible powers, blessings, glory, and love of the unsearchable God, may become visible, sensible, and manifest in it and by it.

' Look at all the variety of creatures; they are what they are for this only end, that in their infinite variety, degrees, and capacities, they may be as so many speaking figures, living forms of the manifold riches and powers of nature, as so many sounds and voices, preachers and trumpets, giving glory and praise and thanksgiving to that Deity of love, which gives life to all nature and creature.

' For every creature of unfallen nature, call it by what name you will, has its form, and power, and state, and place in nature, for no other end but to open and enjoy, to manifest and rejoice in some share of the love, and happiness, and goodness of the Deity, as springing forth in the boundless height and depth of nature [1].'

To turn, once more, from theology to literature : Rousseau and Goethe typically exemplify the kind of men whose religious conceptions, though of the vaguest, are profoundly influenced by nature; but

[1] Law, *Spirit of Love*, ii.

the best, as being the extreme instances of this
class that can possibly be quoted for our purpose,
are Byron and Shelley ; men who but for nature
might have been wholly irreligious, and who therefore exhibit nature's influence in its simplest form,
as being exercised on minds which not only brought
no religious element to its interpretation, but by their
rejection of all positive religion were biassed in an
opposite direction.   Yet they are full of the mystic
emotion which natural sights and sounds inspire.

Take the opening passage, for instance, of Shelley's
Alastor :—

' Earth, ocean, air, beloved brotherhood !
  If our great mother has imbued my soul
  With aught of natural piety to feel
  Your love, and recompense the boon with mine ;
  If dewy morn, and odorous noon, and even,
  With sunset and its gorgeous ministers,
  And solemn midnight's tingling silentness ;
  If autumn's hollow sighs in the sere wood,
  And winter robing with pure snow and crowns
  Of starry ice the gray grass and bare boughs ;
  If spring's voluptuous pantings, when she breathes
  Her first sweet kisses, have been dear to me ;
  If no bright bird, insect, or gentle beast
  I consciously have injured, but still loved
  And cherished these my kindred ;—then forgive
  This boast, beloved brethren, and withdraw
  No portion of your wonted favour now !

Mother of this unfathomable world!
Favour my solemn song, for I have loved
Thee ever, and thee only [1].'

Or again, Byron's lines in *Childe Harold*:—

'To sit on rocks, to muse o'er flood and fell,
To slowly trace the forest's shady scene,
Where things that own not man's dominion dwell,
And mortal foot hath ne'er, or rarely been;
To climb the trackless mountain all unseen,
With the wild flock that never needs a fold;
Alone o'er steeps and foaming falls to lean;
This is not solitude; 'tis but to hold
Converse with nature's charms, and view her stores
    unroll'd [2].'

'Then stirs the feeling infinite, so felt
In solitude, where we are *least* alone;
A truth, which through our being then doth melt,
And purifies from self: it is a tone,
The soul and source of music, which makes known
Eternal harmony [3].'

'I love not man the less, but nature more,
From these our interviews, in which I steal
From all I may be, or have been before,
To mingle with the universe, and feel
What I can ne'er express, yet cannot all conceal [4].'

[1] Shelley, *Alastor.*   [2] Byron, *Childe Harold*, ii. 25.
[3] Ib. iii. 90.   [4] Ib. iv. 178.

But our quotations must, by this time, have grown tedious, so with one passage from Wordsworth we will conclude—the well-known passage in the lines on *Tintern*, which may be called the *locus classicus* upon the subject :—

> ' I have felt
> A presence that disturbs me with the joy
> Of elevated thoughts ; a sense sublime
> Of something far more deeply interfused,
> Whose dwelling is the light of setting suns,
> And the round ocean and the living air,
> And the blue sky, and in the mind of man :
> A motion and a spirit, that impels
> All thinking things, all objects of all thought,
> And rolls through all things. Therefore am I still
> A lover of the meadows and the woods,
> And mountains ; and of all that we behold
> From this green earth ; of all the mighty world
> Of eye and ear,—both what they half create,
> And what perceive ; well pleased to recognize
> In nature and the language of the sense,
> The anchor of my purest thoughts, the nurse,
> The guide, the guardian of my heart, and soul
> Of all my moral being [1].'

Now it will be noticed that the above quotations range through the whole of recorded history ; they might have been indefinitely multiplied ; and every

[1] Wordsworth, *Lines on Tintern Abbey*.

one of them expresses, not the experience of an individual, but of endless generations of men; psalmists, poets, and even philosophers only becoming popular, as they utter the innermost feelings of humanity at large. Here then we have evidence that nature—the material world with its sights and sounds—has exerted, throughout all ages, a profound religious influence on the thoughts and affections of men. There are famous exceptions, of course, like Lucretius; but they are critical and reflective rather than spontaneous; and by the fact that they are recognized as exceptions—paradoxical opponents of habitual opinion —they conduce, if anything, to prove the rule. It should further be borne in mind that the influence in question is independent of any particular theological interpretation; co-existing alike with monotheism, polytheism, pantheism—a mystic emotion, more fundamental than the varieties of creed—a primary, permanent, worldwide agent, in the education of the human soul. Thus matter has, as a fact, from the very dawn of human history, ministered to the religious development of spirit; and when we remember what religion is, and all that it has done for man, it is not too much to say that among all the ministries of matter, this, its service to religion, is beyond comparison the chief.

CHAPTER III

DIVINE IMMANENCE IN NATURE

WE have seen, in the foregoing survey, that the religious influence of external nature is a fact of experience; nothing rare or exceptional, but an ordinary fact of normal human experience. And as the significance of this fact depends upon its magnitude,—its agelong existence and world-wide extent,—it is very important to bear in mind the distinction between the experience itself and its interpretations. For its interpretations being inevitably coloured by the spirit of their age, have varied with every variety of culture and of creed. And as men easily tend to confuse the original impression with the philosophic or theological belief into which they instinctively translate it, they often appear to be going further than their premises allow, and so bring the whole process into disrepute. One man, for example, claims to see in nature a benevolent creator; another a dualism; another a plurality of spiritual beings; another a

E

universally diffused spirit. But all these are interpretations of an immediate experience in the light
of a general belief; and are liable to obscure, by
their contradictory character, the universality of
the experience in question. Still, beneath them
all that experience remains; a sense, in the presence of nature, of contact with something spiritual;
a sense of affinity, or kinship, as the Neo-platonists
described it, with the material world, implying
spirituality within or behind it. The feeling is
hard to describe in more definite terms, since even
the emotions that it arouses are very different in
different minds; but though undefinable it is intense, and, as we have seen, unquestionably normal
to humanity.

Now unless this experience can be discredited,
it must be recognized as weighty evidence of a
spiritual reality behind material things. And it
can only be discredited either by proof that it is
an illusion, or by proof that the faculties which feel
it are unworthy of trust.

To say that it is an illusion is of course equivalent
to saying that it arises from an instinctive inference,
which the growth of knowledge has enabled us to
correct. The world as scientifically understood in
the present day, is very different from the world as
sensibly perceived; and the former is in consequence often supposed to be more real than the
latter—atoms, energy, and ether,—that is to say,

more real than the lights and shadows which their
movements cast.   Hence the emotions, it is argued,
which sensible phenomena arouse have no adequate
counterpart in fact; and as being founded on unreal
appearances must needs be themselves unreal.

This objection at once raises the question, 'what
do we mean by reality?' and this is more easily
asked than answered.   In a sense—and perhaps
this would be the most ordinary answer—whatever
exists is real: a real thing is a thing that actually
exists.   But as soon as we have said this we see
that the problem has only been transferred from
'reality' to 'existence.' For dreams exist; hallucina-
tions exist ; love exists ; the external world exists ;
but with very different kinds or degrees of existence.   Existence therefore must be more defined, if
it is to be our criterion of reality.   And this has
led to the popular opinion, supported by much
popular philosophy, that reality is constituted by
existence in space : in accordance with which, what
were called the primary qualities of bodies, that is
their spacial characteristics, such as size and shape,
came to be regarded as more real than their secondary qualities, such as temperature, colour, or scent.
But this distinction does not help us, for it is
utterly untenable, and together with the view of
reality which it implied is fast becoming obsolete.
On the one hand, all sensations, inasmuch as
they are affections of our bodily organism, exist

equally in space, the redness of an apple, as well as its roundness: while, on the other hand, all sensations alike require mental acts of inference and interpretation, to convert them into perceptions or sources of knowledge. Hence it is impossible to make 'reality' turn upon any distinction between inward and outward, or as it is commonly called, subjective and objective existence; for the simple reason that these two phases, or aspects, of being perpetually interpenetrate and pass into each other, and though separable by mental abstraction, are inseparable in fact.

But if for spacial we substitute personal existence we are at once on a more hopeful road. For, whatever our use of language, there can be no doubt that, in actual life, every man regards his own personality as the most real thing that he knows; not only because its existence is most certain, but because its content is most rich and full. 'I profess,' as Browning says,—

'To know just one fact—my self-consciousness—
'Twixt ignorance and ignorance enisled[1].'

By a natural and instinctive process we extend this conviction to other persons, and regard them as more real than impersonal things. Hence, however little we may have reflected upon it, personality is, as a matter of fact, our tacitly acknowledged

[1] Browning, *Francis Furini*.

standard of reality ; and other things are accounted real, in proportion as they are related to, and so embraced within, the sphere of personality. Thus my friends and neighbours, my property, the books that I have read, the science that I have acquired, the deeds that I have done, the things that gratify my senses, or offer resistance to my muscles, 'my star that dartles the red and the blue,' are more real to me than all the world beside, with which as yet I have only negative relations. In a word what affects me personally, and thereby becomes part of myself, is real for me ; while what affects me most persistently and most powerfully is most real. I recognize the same to be the case with other persons ; that each has his own world of reality : and further that, while some things only affect individuals, and may therefore be called subjectively or relatively real ; other things affect all alike, and are therefore real for all, that is to say universally or objectively real. And when I correct my subjective impressions, by reference to objective reality, it is this that I mean by the term, not what is external, but what appeals equally to all. For 'what appears to all,' as Aristotle says, 'that we say exists' (ὃ πᾶσι δοκεῖ τοῦτ' εἶναι φαμέν). Now the condition of this 'appearing to all' is presentation in external space, since even a thought, if it is to appear to all, must be written in a book. Consequently space is a medium, but not therefore

a constituent of reality. Thus we consider a word
more real than a thought, and a deed than a word ;
and this is because they successively involve more
of our entire personality. In uttering and enacting
our thoughts, we have the courage of our opinions ;
we put our will into them and show that we mean
them ; and therefore that they are real for us.
While at the same time, through the medium of
utterance, or bodily expression, we bring them into
contact with other persons, and thus enlarge the
sphere of their reality. So when a man writes
a book, carves a statue, paints a picture, he is said
to realize his thoughts or make them real; not
merely because he externalizes them in space ; but
because he puts his will into them ; changing the
creations of his mere imagination into creations of
his very self; while, in so doing, he also publishes
them, or makes them public ; that is he recreates
them in the minds and affections of countless other
persons.

Objection is sometimes made to our admitting
degrees of reality; but there is abundant philosophical authority for so doing; and if reality is to
imply existence, it must, as we have seen, vary in
degree. It follows that personality, the highest
form of existence which we know, must be our
standard of reality; and if so, what is most intimately and permanently connected with personality
must be for us, that is for the world of persons,

correspondingly real. Things are real, not in proportion as they are independent of us, or removed
from us, but in proportion, on the contrary, as they
are related to us: their removal in space only
making them more real, because it invests them
with a permanent possibility of relationship to a
larger number of persons. Hence, to return to our
starting-point, atoms and their properties, as revealed by science, are not more real than the sensible impressions which they create in all normally
constituted persons: while those impressions which
profoundly touch the feelings, and modify the conduct of innumerable men, may even be called more
real, in the only intelligible sense of the word, than
their mechanical causes, known only to a small
minority of the race.

Take the sunset for example—a series of etherial
vibrations, merely mechanical in origin, and, as such,
other than they seem ; whose total effect is to create
in us an optical illusion, making the sun, and not
the earth, appear to move. Yet, as men watch its
appearance, thoughts and feelings arise in their
hearts, that move their inmost being in unnumbered
ways. Youth is fired with high ideals ; age con-
soled with peaceful hopes ; saints, as they pray, see
heaven opened ; sinners feel conscience strangely
stirred.   Mourners are comforted ; weary ones
rested ; artists inspired ; lovers united ; worldlings
purified and softened as they gaze. In a short half-

hour all is over: the mechanical process has come to an end; the gold has melted into grey. But countless souls, meanwhile, have been soothed, and solaced, and uplifted by that evening benediction from the far-off sky; and the course of human life to-day is modified and moulded by the setting of yesterday's sun. In the same way, a piece of music, a sonata or a symphony, is more real to its audience than the acoustic laws which cause it, or the instruments upon which it is performed. The world of science, in other words, is no more real than the world of sense; the two being only different aspects of one continuous whole, of which the human organism is also a part. It follows that we have no ground whatever for discounting the religious influence of external nature, as less real than the mechanical phenomena, on which physically speaking it depends, and of which, in fact, it may be called a manifestation. The two things impress different faculties in us, but with equal justification.

This leads us to the second objection above-mentioned. which is really the same objection, urged from another point of view; the untrustworthiness, namely, of our emotions. It is too often assumed that the emotions, as contrasted with the intellect, are untrustworthy guides to truth; and many even of those who think otherwise, still allow the emotions to be called irrational; as though belief in them were an act of faith, in some sort needing an apology.

Thus, in the present case, the prospect of nature confessedly fills us with emotion ; but such emotion, it is argued, has no right to be its own interpreter ; no right to assure us of its contact with a spiritual object ; no right, in a word, to give us any knowledge, beyond that of its own existence. Now this sharp distinction between feeling and understanding, the emotions and the intellect, is wholly artificial, and untrue to fact. Knowledge starts neither with mere understanding, nor mere feeling, both of which are abstractions, but with personal experience ; the experience of a person who both thinks and feels, and in whose unity thought and feeling are inseparably fused and blent. 'When the soul feels, it is called sense . . . when it understands it is called mind,' as Alcuin admirably put it long ago. Experience begins with sensation, that is to say, feeling ; but sensation, as we have seen, no sooner begins to be felt, than it begins to be interpreted by thought ; while thought itself, the critic and interpreter, is the thought of a being full of feelings, which in one degree or another qualify every process of his mind. It is true that we can isolate parts of our personal experience, by exclusive attention, and make them objects of independent pursuit ; but this always involves a process of limitation, or abstraction, which in proportion to its completeness removes us from the totality of truth. Thus a tea-taster, or a piano-tuner, confines his attention to particular sensations; a pure mathematician to abstract thought; while an artist will employ different faculties from a soldier, and a soldier from a judge. And it is very easy to be so biassed by our special occupations, that we become incomplete, one-sided, fragmentary men, like Wordsworth's philosopher—

'One that would peep and botanize
Upon his mother's grave.

.   .   .   .

One to whose smooth rubbed soul can cling
Nor form, nor feeling, great nor small;
A reasoning, self-sufficing thing,
An intellectual all in all[1].'

But the way in which common sense always resents such specialism is sufficient proof of our instinctive feeling that, after all, we are persons and not machines; and as persons we confront not a part only of our environment, but the whole. The plain man as well as the philosopher, has and must have his theory of life, however little he may put it into words; his view that is to say of his relations to the whole of his surroundings; nature, society, and for all who believe in Him, God. But the whole of our surroundings, our total environment, impresses and appeals to our total personality; that is to say, to our personality not regarded as a group of separate faculties, but as a unity or whole. Consequently it

[1] Wordsworth, *A Poet's Epitaph.*

can only be apprehended aright by our total personality, our whole self with its complex interaction of emotion, intellect, and will; in which persistent feeling is as important an element as consistent thought.

Reason is of course always at work to understand the world, and by that very fact implies its belief that the world is, in the last resort, intelligible, or capable of being ultimately understood; and its consequent right to reject what is demonstrably irrational or contradictory of reason. But things may be unintelligible, in the sense that we do not now understand them, without being in any way irrational or intrinsically absurd. The world indeed is full of such unintelligible things—things of whose nature we know nothing, but of whose reality we are sure; and a rational man accepts them as facts, however unable he may be to explain them. We are familiar enough with this principle in ordinary life, where we daily accept and utilize facts, which, though scientifically explicable, we ourselves do not personally understand. A plain man does not understand his sensations of hunger and thirst or heat and cold, but when he accepts them as facts, and feeds and clothes himself accordingly, he is as rational as the physiologist who has a complete understanding of all the processes of animal life. And the same is the case with things which are at present beyond all human comprehension. Time, space,

motion, life, love, and indeed the whole of our experience, in its last analysis, is inexplicable. We are
obliged to accept it as a fact, before we can reason
about it at all; and no amount of subsequent reasoning can ever explain how it came to be a fact.
Hence reason, in all concrete cases, has to deal with
materials which it never fully understands; and its
action is limited accordingly. It is like a discoverer
who can assert that what he has found exists, but
cannot add that what he has not found does not
exist. In discussing any part of our personal experience, therefore, the first question that arises, is,
not whether it is rational, but whether it is a fact.
If it is a fact, if it exists, if it is really there, reason
cannot set it aside, for any present inability to understand it. And this is precisely the condition of the
particular experience before us. It is a fact as old
as history; normal and natural to man; and to discredit it, as merely emotional, because we cannot
explain it, is absurd. It is not merely emotional;
it is personal : it is the effect, that is to say, of the
natural world, not upon our feelings, abstracted
from the rest of us, but upon our feelings in their
vital connexion with the rest of our personality.
And in this connexion we have as much justification
for trusting our feelings as for trusting our reason;
since in either case it is the one personality behind
them which we really trust. If I trust my reason,
I am trusting one function of my complex per-

sonality; that is to say, I am trusting my personality in one of its activities. And when, by so doing, I reach results which can be verified, as for instance in the discovery of a new planet, I prove my trust to be justifiable. I prove that my personality to that extent acts truly. But this very fact inevitably leads me to conclude that the other functions of the same personality, its other modes of activity, must be equally veracious; and that feelings which are natural and normal, may be trusted in evidence of what they feel; for in either case it is one self-same personality that acts. I might be sceptical, if I could suppose that my whole personality misled me; but science, by proving that part of my personality tells the truth, banishes this supposition, and makes scepticism impossible. Henceforth I must trust my personality, and if in one of its functions, then in all, for they stand or fall together.

Returning, then, to the point from which we started, the religious influence of external nature; this cannot, we see, be discredited on the ground that the sights and sounds on which it rests are illusory—mere phenomena—mere appearances; for the very fact of the effect which they produce in us is their sufficient title to reality. It is precisely because they appear, and by appearing profoundly affect us, that they are real. Neither can the influence in question be disparaged for being emotional rather than rational; since there is no possible ground for elevating one element of our personality above another, or above the action, which is what here occurs, of our personality as a whole.

But if all this be true, and the experience in question cannot be invalidated, then it remains, a stupendous evidence that the material universe is a manifestation of spirit. This question is too often treated as if it were merely an argumentative inference—an inference from beauty, or the need of causation, or the traces of design, or the like; in oblivion of the fact that behind, and prior to, all these inferences, there is the spiritual influence, which nature does, as we have seen, undoubtedly exert. And our reason for emphasizing the distinction between this influence and its interpretations, is to bring its universality into stronger relief. However variously men interpret it, they all feel and have ever felt it alike.

Now we often hear it said that the first aspect of nature—its *prima facie* aspect—makes for materialism. But in the light of the foregoing facts, this is unquestionably not the case. The *prima facie* aspect of the world conduces to spiritual belief, and the view which makes for materialism is not the *prima facie* view, but that which we obtain by going behind the *prima facie* view, to examine its machinery. But in so doing we pass from the whole to a partial view. The *prima facie* view is the judgement of our personality as a whole, in contact with nature as a whole; that is, a judgement in which our entire being takes part. But the analytical or scientific view is a partial view, with important elements left out; it makes abstraction, for its own purpose, of certain properties of things, and omits the remainder. And though the physical sciences have been called concrete, in comparison with the still more abstract mathematics, yet they are all abstract to this extent, that they regard only the physical relations of phenomena, which possess also moral and emotional relations. Such abstraction is of course as necessary for the development of thought, as is its practical equivalent, the division of labour, for the development of life. As social progress only begins, when the different members of a society confine themselves to the performance of different functions; so intellectual progress only begins, when the various aspects of the world are distributed for analysis, each to a separate science. But neither the specialization of science, nor the division of labour, are ends in themselves. If we wish to understand human nature, in its fullness, we do not confine our attention to particular classes of the community— soldiers, statesmen, merchants, thinkers, artists, artisans; but pass on to the total society, which includes, and is enriched by all these partial lives; and supplements, and correlates, and unifies them all. In the same way, if we wish to understand material nature, in its fullness, we must pass on from its partial analysis to its total effect; from the examination of its mechanical structure, its chemical properties, its organic development, its aesthetic appearance, to the actual result of all these things in synthesis, that is, in their living combination, as presented to the personality of man. We then find that nature, in its concrete unity, has a spiritual character which cannot be discovered from its abstract parts; any more than the subject of a puzzle picture can be known before we have put its isolated portions together; or the meaning of a word before we have arranged its letters when given us to spell. In order to emphasize the fact that this spirituality of nature is not an inference but an experience, we have purposely, as above stated, set the variety of its interpretations aside; though that very variety is of course additional proof of the reality of the experience in question; since it shows that, however differing in all their theories of the world, men have always agreed that here was a fact, a persistent something, to be explained. But now that we are clear upon this point, we may return to the further question of its interpretation. What is the relation of the material universe to that Spirit of which it so persistently seems to speak? The experience with which we are dealing has, as we have seen, been historically compatible with theories of every description ; but those theories are not all equally tenable on other grounds.

Polytheism and dualism, for instance, are no longer possible interpretations ; for the universe is obviously one. Its unity of structure and development, though often maintained in other ages, has been placed by modern science in an entirely new light ; and that unity leaves no place for the thought of contradictory beings at its helm. If the system of things be guided by spiritual power, that power must be ultimately one. And if we are to form any further conjecture of the way in which this Spirit is related to the material order, we must recur to the starting-point of all our knowledge, namely, ourselves. Human personality, however little we may comprehend it, is yet the thing that we know best, as being the only thing that we know at first hand, and from within. And further, human personality exhibits spirit and matter in combination ; such intimate combination that, as we have seen above, they do not admit of being completely sundered. It is in human personality alone, therefore, that we must look for light upon our subject ; the limited light indeed of a lantern carried in our own uncertain hand, but still the only light that we can possibly possess.

Now we find on reflection that what we call our spirit transcends, or is, in a sense, independent of the bodily organism on which otherwise it so entirely depends. Metaphysically speaking this is seen in our self-consciousness, or power of separating our self as subject from our self as object, a thing wholly inconceivable as the result of any material process, and relating us at once to an order of being which we are obliged to call immaterial. But as metaphysical analysis is ' caviare to the general,' while the metaphysically-minded will find this point amply illustrated by most modern philosophers, it will be sufficient for our purpose to appeal to the more familiar field of morals.

Morally speaking, we are responsible for our actions. That is a fact which no sane man doubts. It is the assumption on which the whole course of our political and social life is carried on; and if a man takes leave to deny it, except in theory, law soon interferes for his correction. There is no fact in the world that, in their misery, men would more gladly have denied; yet they are agreed to treat its denial as a manifest absurdity. Surely, then, it is as strong a conviction as any that can be conceived. And this conviction is amply sufficient for our purpose; for it implies that we are self-identical and free, the same personal unit to-day that we were when born—whereas all the matter of our bodies has changed—and capable of determining ourselves from within, whereas all matter is determined by something else, and from

without [1].   Our present object is not to argue these
points, which have been argued abundantly elsewhere, but simply to refer to them, as results of
past argument, in illustration of the fact that, with
all our dependence upon matter, we yet transcend
it ; we move in a plane above it, and are, though
in a limited degree, its masters and not its slaves.
This, then, is one aspect of the relation between
spirit and matter, as known within the circle of our
own personality.   And when we pass beyond that
circle to mould the external world to our use, through
various forms of scientific invention, and artistic
creation, it becomes still more apparent that spirit
has a dominant and transcendent relation to matter.

But from another point of view our spirit may be
described as 'immanent' in matter.   It not only
works through the brain and nervous system, but,
as a result, pervades the entire organism, animating
and inspiring it with its own 'peculiar difference';
so that we recognize a man's character in the
expression of his eye, the tone of his voice, the
touch of his hand; his unconscious and instinctive
postures, and gestures, and gait.   Nor is this 'immanence' confined to the bodily organism.   It extends,
in what may be called a secondary degree, to the
inanimate objects of the external world.   For a
man imprints his spiritual character upon all the
things with which he deals, his house, his clothes,

[1] See Appendix.

his furniture, the various products of his hand or head. And when we speak of a man's spirit surviving in his works, the expression is no mere metaphor; for through those works, even though dead and gone, he continues to influence his fellow-men. And when we look at the pictures of Raffaelle, or listen to the music of Beethoven, or read the poetry of Dante, or the philosophy of Plato, the spirit of the great Masters is affecting us as really as if we saw them face to face : it is immanent in the painted canvas and the printed page.

Spirit then, as we know it in our own personal experience, has two different relations to matter, that of transcendence, and that of immanence. But though logically distinct, these two relations are not actually separate ; they are two aspects of one fact; two points of view from which the single action of our one personality may be regarded. As self-conscious, self-identical, self-determined, we possess qualities which transcend or rise above the laws of matter; but we can only realize these qualities, and so become aware of them, by acting in the material world ; while conversely material objects—our bodies, and our works of art—could never possibly be regarded as expressions of spirit, if spirit were not at the same time recognized as distinct from its medium of manifestation.

If then we are to raise the question, 'what is the relation of the supreme Spirit to the material universe?' this is the analogy upon which we must proceed; for we have no other. We may indeed decline the problem as wholly insoluble; but if we attempt its solution at all, it must of necessity be upon the lines of the only experience which we possess—this experience in which transcendence and immanence are combined.

This at once excludes pantheism, the belief that God is merely immanent in matter; for attractive as this creed has often seemed to worshippers of nature, it cannot really be construed into thought. Spirit which is merely immanent in matter, without also transcending it, cannot be spirit at all; it is only another aspect of matter, having neither self-identity nor freedom. Pantheism is thus really indistinguishable from materialism; it is merely materialism grown sentimental, but no more tenable for its change of name.

The logical opposite of pantheism is deism, in the sense of belief in a merely transcendent God; and this is equally inconsistent with our analogy; for as we have no experience whatever of spirit or matter as existing apart, we cannot conceive either term of the deistic universe. But deism of this kind, though it has occupied an important place in history, is scarcely a form of thought with which at the present day we need to reckon. It belongs to a metaphysical rather than a scientific atmosphere and age.

Yet another view of the question has been suggested under the name of monism; the view that
'matter in motion is substantially identical with
mind,' that they are two aspects of one thing, which
from the outside we call matter, and from the inside
mind.   At first sight this seems only another name
for materialism; and, in fact, the word monism is
expressly used by Haeckel as synonymous with
scientific materialism.   But its use has also been
advocated in a theistic sense; the mental aspect
being regarded as prior in importance, though not
in existence to the material,—a position very much
akin to Spinozism.   Now the supposed advantage of
this theory is, that it abolishes all the difficulties
of dualism.   But it is obviously no more than an
imaginative conjecture, and upon what does it rest?
'We have only to suppose that the antithesis between mind and motion—subject and object—is
itself phenomenal or apparent, not absolute or real[1].'
That is to say that, when we are confronted in our
personal experience with a dualism, whose mystery
we cannot solve, we may at once attain intellectual
satisfaction, by the simple expedient of assuming it
to be an illusion.   But this is precisely what the
materialist does, and is condemned for doing; and
we are no more justified in discrediting the primary
facts of consciousness in the interests of spirit, than
in the interests of matter.   Monism, in short, whether

[1] Romanes, *Mind, Matter, and Monism.*

material or spiritual, is not based upon what we know in ourselves, and what is, to that extent, solid fact; but upon distrust of what we think we know in ourselves—a sceptical foundation, which cannot possibly support a positive conclusion. It should further be noticed that, in the above quotation, mind and matter are treated as synonymous with subject and object. This in itself is a mistake, but a mistake essential to the theory. For it is only by considering mind as a mere series of subjective or mental states, that we can plausibly consider motion as its parallel concomitant. But the characteristic of mind, as we know it in our personal spirit, is that it is both subject and object at once; it is capable of becoming its own object, and saying I am I. It is through this power of self-consciousness, or self-diremption, that spirit transcends matter, as we have already had occasion to point out; and it is precisely this power which we are unable to conceive as having any material equivalent. Monism, in fact, started from the physical side, from analysis of the cerebral conditions of thought; it rests on physical analogies, and is coloured by physical modes of thought; and the attempt to make it metaphysically tenable seems an impossible *tour de force*.

It remains then that we confine ourselves to the analogy of our personal experience, and conceive of God as at once transcending and immanent in

nature; for however incomprehensible this relationship may be, we know it in our own case to be
a fact, and may legitimately infer its analogue
outside ourselves.

On this analogy then, the divine presence which
we recognize in nature will be the presence of
a Spirit, which infinitely transcends the material
order, yet sustains and indwells it the while. We
cannot indeed explain the method, either of the
transcendence, or of the indwelling; but we come
no nearer to an explanation, by attempting, with
any of the above-mentioned theories, to obtain
simplicity by suppressing either aspect of the only
analogy that we possess. But it will be remembered that in our own case we noticed two degrees
of immanence; our essential immanence in our
body, which is consequently often called our
person; and our contingent immanence in the
works which we are free to create or not at will.
The question therefore inevitably arises, under
which of these analogies are we to think of God's
relation to the world. Is the universe His body,
or His work? Different answers have been given
to this question by different thinkers; and it is
obvious that no answer can be more than conjectural or hypothetical.

Under these circumstances we are entitled to
urge, that the Trinitarian conception of God, which
we Christians have independent reasons for believ-

ing to be true, is intellectually the most satisfactory; since it embraces both the kinds of immanence in question, and therefore harmonizes with the entire analogy of our personal experience. For according to this doctrine, the Second Person of the Trinity is the essential, adequate, eternal manifestation of the First, 'the express image of His person,' 'in whom dwelleth the fulness of the Godhead bodily,' while ' by Him all things were made.' Here then we have our two degrees of immanence; the complete immanence of the Father in the Son, of which our own relation to our body is an inadequate type; and, as a result of this, His immanence in creation, analogous to our presence in our works; with the obvious difference, of course, that we finite beings who die and pass away, can only be impersonally present in our works; whereas He must be conceived as ever present to sustain and animate the universe, which thus becomes a living manifestation of Himself;—no mere machine, or book, or picture, but a perpetually sounding voice.

CHAPTER IV

DIVINE IMMANENCE IN MAN

THE thought of God's immanence in nature has commended itself at the present day, on quite independent grounds, to many of the students both of science and philosophy. But if God is immanent in nature, He must also be immanent in man, since man is a part of nature; and if it is not so, our previous belief will be discredited, while if it is so, it will be strongly confirmed.

Now when we turn to man, we are struck at once by the phenomenon of conscience: the most mysterious of all his attributes. What we commonly call conscience is a complex thing; various strands are woven into its woof. It has a long history behind it, and was not, in early ages, either as intelligent or as definite as now; nor, of course, is it equally educated among all races at the present day. But what we find in its highest development must have been implicitly present in its earliest germ; and what we do find is a sense, within our inmost self, of something 'not ourself

which makes for righteousness'; a categorical imperative, an authoritative voice, which we can only
ascribe to God. This is the religious account of
conscience, and it cannot be explained away. No
hypothesis that has ever been suggested will really
account for its unique authority; and moreover we
have not to deal with past possibilities, but present
facts. We know perfectly well what we mean by a
categorical imperative, an absolute, unqualified, unconditional command; and we know perfectly well
that it is thus, and only thus, that conscience speaks.
And it is this that leads us to regard conscience

'As God's most intimate Presence in the soul
And His most perfect Image in the world[1].'

Moreover in proportion as conscience is consis-
tently obeyed, goodness and holiness of character
result; and this is a process which the good and
holy, the men who by experience know most about
it, habitually ascribe to the co-operation of God,
—'God working within them,' in scriptural phrase,
'both to will and to do of His good pleasure.'
'*Amor Dei intellectualis,*' says even Spinoza, '*pars
est infiniti amoris, quo Deus seipsum amat,*' 'Our
love of God in its highest form is but a portion of
God's infinite love for Himself.' It is easy to say
that such men misinterpret their own history, and
attribute to divine assistance what is but a function

[1] Wordsworth, *Excursion*, iv.

of themselves. But those who have confessedly succeeded in attaining what other men have failed to attain, must, in common sense, be credited with knowing best what has been the secret of their own success. Nor as a matter of fact is the experience in question at all confined to the saintly few, the elect minority in every age, who have been eminent for character and conduct. It is echoed and has been echoed, from the dawn of history, in countless human hearts ; far and wide men have believed that, in the spiritual struggles of their inner life, they were aware of divine intervention and assistance ; while in proportion as the struggle has been more successful, the conviction has grown more sure. The fact that such a phenomenon cannot be expressed in scientific terms, and is entirely out of the range of our psychology, must not be allowed to blind us to its enormous magnitude—the immense place which it fills, and has filled in the spiritual life of our race.

Thus God's immanence in nature, we may reasonably assert, reappears as inspiration in man. Meanwhile our spiritual character reacts upon the material instrument of its realization, moulding the brain and nervous system, and thence the entire bodily organism, into gradual accordance with itself; till the expression of the eye, the lines of the face, the tones of the voice, the touch of the hand, the movements, and manners, and gracious demeanour, all reveal, with increasing clearness, the nature of the spirit that has made them what they are. Thus the interior beauty of holiness comes by degrees to be a visible thing ; and through His action upon our spirit, God is made manifest in our flesh. While in proportion as we are enabled to recognize this progressive manifestation of God in matter, we are prepared to find it culminate in His actual Incarnation, the climax of His immanence in the world.

It must not of course be forgotten that one of the popular objections to Christianity is founded upon this very fact ; that it is so congruous with human thought. Man, we know, in uncritical ages, tends to believe in incarnations; they are a common form of thought with him ; he is predisposed in their favour ; medicine men, priests, kings. prophets, and abnormal individuals of every kind, being constantly regarded as embodied gods. And the Christian Incarnation, it is argued, is but the last lingering survival of these obsolete modes of thought. Its resemblance to countless other baseless beliefs of the kind creates a presumption that it is not true. This argument is usually answered by a reference to history ; to the external evidence and internal character of the Christian story, as contrasted with all other accounts of incarnations. But as many minds are prevented, by the very argument in question, from approaching the facts of history without antecedent bias, it may be well to notice that there is a logical as well as an historical answer.

The tendency to believe in incarnations involves two elements—a belief in their probability, and a belief in their actual occurrence; a belief that they may happen any day, and a belief that they have happened here and now; the one being a general principle of thought, and the other a particular judgement of fact. And it is obvious that no number of mistakes on this latter point would affect the credibility of a new instance. The mere fact that a possible event did not happen, in ninety-nine supposed cases, is no reason for arguing that it will not happen in the hundredth,—as the familiar story of the boy and the wolf may suffice to show.

It is therefore with the other element that the argument is concerned, the general tendency to believe incarnations probable. But a general tendency in the human mind to expect a thing cannot possibly be twisted into a presumption against its occurrence. 'Men were always expecting it, therefore it cannot have occurred,' is, when baldly stated, a manifest absurdity. Of course it will be answered that what is meant is 'Men were always expecting it, therefore they invented its occurrence.' But the fact of the expectation does not logically make invention a likelier alternative than occurrence; except upon one hypothesis,

namely, that the occurrence is impossible. And
here we have the root of the whole matter. An
incarnation is first ruled out of court, as being
a priori impossible; and then the expectation of it
is treated as an illusion. But this is what logicians
call begging the question. That is to say, the
tendency to believe in incarnations creates no presumption whatever against the reality of a particular
incarnation, except upon the previous assumption
that the tendency is false. Thus the argument
before us does not really rest upon the fact in
human nature which it quotes, but upon a purely
arbitrary interpretation of the fact. We may say
baldly and boldly, 'incarnations are impossible';
but we cannot strengthen the statement by adding
'because mankind has always believed them.' An
assumption may look more plausible when disguised
as an induction, but it does not therefore gain
logical force.

Nor is this negative conclusion all that we are
justified in drawing. For when fairly faced, the
tendency in question is not only no argument
against the Incarnation, but rather creates a presumption of its truth. For it is only part and
parcel of man's general sense of the divine nearness
—nearness to and interest in himself. Man's
habitual, and almost instinctive belief in the existence of a God or gods, has always been regarded
as among the strongest evidences of natural reli-

gion. Its universality, that is to say, has been
recognized as weighty evidence of its truth. But
almost everywhere we find this belief to be inseparably connected with the further conviction, that
their gods desire intercourse and friendship with
men. And if the universality of the one belief is
recognized as an argument in its favour, the practical universality of the other must be so too; it
must be regarded as pointing to a truth. Again,
we recognize that the religious instinct, in its earlier
stages, continually misinterpreted itself — finding
gods in stocks and stones, sun, moon, and stars,
birds, beasts, and fishes. But we do not consider
the instinct itself as discredited by the fact, or our
present conception of God as less true, because it
was only slowly disentangled from these absurdities.
It was not the religious instinct, we consider, that
erred, but the crude philosophy which could not
interpret the instinct. And it would seem to have
been the same with the special tendency that we
are considering. Men took it for granted that
their gods were desirous of intercourse with them;
and this instinctive expectation made it easy to
believe, that among other modes of manifestation,
the gods had not only spoken through inspired
men, but had themselves from time to time assumed
human form, either in the way of theophany or
incarnation. But here again no number of mistaken facts can invalidate the instinct behind them.

Folklore and mythology find endless traces of supposed incarnations which are quite as unspiritual, and even immoral, as they are unscientific; and conflict not only with all canons of rational criticism, but even with the ordinary dictates of plain common sense. Yet these fictions only emphasize the persistence of the instinct which continued to invent them, because it continued to demand them. And when at length we are confronted with a tale of Incarnation, whose spiritual sublimity and actual influence are alike absolutely unique, its believers may fairly recognize in the previous expectation of mankind, an additional proof of its truth. The event has occurred, they may reasonably say, which man's prophetic soul divined. The Incarnation, that he often so fantastically dreamed of, has at last become a fact.

But it may still be said, and often is said, that the Incarnation, in which Christians believe, is really as incompatible with reverent notions of God as the unworthier legends to which we have alluded; since it involves a miraculous interference with the order of nature, which is utterly unbecoming of the author of nature; and ought in fact to shock our scientific sense, as the earlier stories shock our moral sense of what is appropriate to the character of God.

This is a very familiar objection, and has still great weight with many minds, but it involves various assumptions which, to say the least, are open to dispute.

In the first place, it involves a false antithesis, as will easily appear from what has gone before, between nature and man. 'Is the great order of nature likely to be altered, it magniloquently asks, in deference to the insignificant interests of man?' But man and nature are inseparable parts of one whole, as we have already seen; and foremost among man's attributes is his belief in his own spiritual importance; the absolute worth of his personality, as against all impersonal things. This instinct may be justified by philosophical analysis, as we have already had occasion to point out; but it is far more vividly vindicated in ordinary eyes, by the martyr who dies for a creed. For martyrdom is the complete refusal to compromise our spiritual consistency, by denying what we believe; the extreme assertion that spiritual integrity outweighs all material things; that at all costs we must remain ourselves, and not contradict ourselves; that our personality has absolute worth. There can be no question whatever that this conviction is inherent in the very make and constitution of man: and as such it is an element in the universe; a phenomenon or part of the universe; and as real as any of its other phenomena or parts. What we find therefore is not an order of nature on the one side, and human interest on the other; but a single system of which this conviction is a part ; an order of nature in which it is included ; a combination of two elements of which one possesses the attribute of claiming supremacy over the other. We cannot study external nature except through our spirit, and our spirit brings this inevitable conviction with it to the task. In the very act of knowing matter we judge it subordinate to spirit, while matter itself subserves the judgement through the brain by which it is made. To say therefore that the order of nature is not likely to be altered for man, or in other words, that matter is not likely to be altered in the interest of spirit, is to contradict our fundamental conception of the relative importance of the two. And no such argument, from moral improbability, can be raised against miracle as such.

Moreover, when the miraculous character of the Incarnation is attacked, it is important to distinguish between the fact of the Incarnation, and its mode, the conditions and circumstances by which it was accompanied. For upon reflection we may easily see, that there is no justification whatever for regarding the fact of the Incarnation, the fact of God becoming man, as a miracle in any ordinary sense of the word. For by a miracle we mean an interference with the usual order of events,—something which happens differently from other cases of its kind,—as when a dead man comes to life again, or water is made wine. But an event which by its nature is, *ex hypothesi*, unique — the sole and only possible occurrence of its kind — has no usual order with which to come in conflict; and unless it be intrinsically irrational, there can be no antecedent presumption against it. It may be strange, surprising, stupendous, but, in no intelligible sense of the word, miraculous. Thus nothing in the course of nature, nothing in the previous history of man, could create a shred of rational presumption against the occurrence of an Incarnation. It stands free to be judged without bias on its own intrinsic claim.

It may of course be replied that this distinction between the fact and the mode of the Incarnation is unfair; since the two things are inseparable elements of one supposed event, which must be discredited as a whole, by the incredible character of either part. But the whole point of the distinction in question is to preclude such an objection, by showing that the fact stands in a necessary relation of logical priority to the mode, and must be considered first: that the Incarnation is the inevitable presupposition of its miracles. If Jesus Christ was the divine Author of our human life and death, it is manifestly absurd to say that He could not, or would not, heal the sick and raise the dead. Such miracles, taken by themselves, would be in the last degree improbable; but as results of an Incarnation they are so probable that we should even call them natural. Thus the incredibility of the mode entirely vanishes, if the fact be true ; and we can never ask about a Christian miracle simply, ' Is it likely to have happened ? ' but ' Is it likely to have happened, if Christ was God ? ' Consequently, when we hear the Gospels rejected on account of their miracles, it is obvious that the divinity of Christ has been rejected first. But if so, upon what ground ? evidently and necessarily upon an *a priori* ground —the *a priori* ground that an Incarnation is improbable. Hence it is important to show, as we have done above, that such a presumption has no logical foundation. It is merely a baseless prejudice for which no sound reason can be produced. For what are the facts of the case? The picturesque simile of the bird flying in from the night, we know not whence, and out in the night again, we know not whither, is as true of human life to-day, as when it was first urged, in the hall of Eadwine, as an argument for listening to the Christian teacher. With all our science, we know nothing, unless from revelation, of the ultimate origin or final destiny of man ; why he exists, and how the purpose of his existence can best be carried out. Even of what man really is, we have probably at present no more knowledge, than an egg would convey of an eagle, or an acorn of an oak. And if this is true of our knowledge of man, it is true *a fortiori* of our knowledge of God.

Apart then altogether from any question of revelation, can there be a shadow of reason for presuming that God, of whose essential nature we are absolutely ignorant, cannot become man, of whose essential nature we know hardly more. It may be as natural, so to speak, for God to become man, as for God to create man ; and the Incarnation may, for all we know, be an inevitable consequence of creation, as some theologians have ventured to assert. Any prejudice therefore that we may feel, against the probability of the Incarnation, is not a reasonable conviction but an irrational bias ; due to the shock of its great mystery upon the mind. We are so unaccustomed to think of mysteries, in the trivial round of daily life, that their unexpected presentation is an affront to us. Yet all ultimate realities are equally mysterious, when once we pause to think of them,—being, life, sense, thought, love, will, God;—*omnia exeunt in mysterium*, as the schoolmen said ; there can be no possible presumption against the occurrence of an event merely because its mystery is profound.

Still, the absence of contrary presumption, it may be urged, does not carry us far ; and there must be very strong evidence in favour of the Incarnation, before it can be received. There is of course very strong evidence, in the judgement of its believers ; but its strength is still often obscured, by the mistaken idea that it consists chiefly of miracles. For

IV]   *DIVINE IMMANENCE IN MAN*   87

miracles, at the present day, far from supporting
anything else, are popularly supposed to be themselves much in need of support; so that, for many
minds, they tend to invalidate, rather than to fortify,
the credit of any document wherein their occurrence
is recorded.   And though this position requires
criticism, it may for the present be passed over;
since miracles neither are, nor ever were regarded
by the Christian Church as, the primary proof of
the Incarnation.   For the Incarnation is primarily
and essentially a spiritual fact, and no conceivable
amount of evidence that was merely material could
prove it; spiritual things must be spiritually discerned.   And so the personality of Jesus Christ is
its own self-evidence. 'Which of you convinceth
Me of sin?' He asks, and 'If I speak the truth, why
do ye not believe Me?'   A sinless man must speak
the truth, and therefore be what He asserts Himself.
He appeals to His character to substantiate His
claim : bids men look at Him and recognize that
He must be what He says.   Now such an appeal
is directly addressed to the spiritual insight of His
hearers, and can only succeed where that insight
exists.   It was rejected as a matter of course by
those who did not know goodness when they saw
it ; the self-satisfied or sensual men who assumed
bad motives for good actions; the morally and
spiritually blind.   But it was accepted by His
faithful followers, His intimate friends of every day;

the men and women whom His glance had kindled, and His voice had quickened to new life ; and in whose souls, as they looked and listened, insight arose out of much love. And it was this inner circle of ' witnesses ' that were gradually trained by Jesus Christ, first to believe in Him, and then to understand Him, and finally to proclaim Him to the world.

This then was the primary proof, the essential evidence of the Incarnation ; the self-revelation of a person to persons. But it was unquestionably accompanied, as Christians believe, by works of superhuman power, and sealed by the crowning miracle of resurrection from the dead. The attempt to deny these miracles, or to reject the Gospels on account of them, lands us amid worse problems than those which it seeks to solve. For we cannot eliminate from history either the person or the work of Christ ; and the more we discredit the recorded account of them, the more hopelessly perplexing does their supremacy become.

But if the Incarnation was a fact, and Jesus Christ was what He claimed to be, His miracles so far from being improbable, will appear the most natural things in the world. For no one will deny, that in this case, He could have worked them ; and when we look at them, it seems likely that He would; for they harmonize completely with His whole character and work,—being mainly acts of charity and mercy, either to the bodies or the souls of men; and at the same time profoundly symbolical of spiritual truth. They are indeed so essentially a part of the character depicted in the Gospels, that without them that character would entirely disappear. They flow naturally from a Person who, despite His obvious humanity, impresses us throughout as being at home in two worlds. Moreover the possessor of these miraculous powers is described as tempted to misuse them. No one, who reads the account of the temptation, can suppose for a moment that it was related with any reference to the credibility of miracles. But for that very reason its indirect bearing on their credibility is great; for nothing can suggest more forcibly that the miraculous power was real, than the statement incidentally made, that it was the subject of temptation; with the further implication that in many cases it was consciously present but unused. The issue also of this temptation tallies, in a very remarkable degree, with the nature of the miracles recorded in the Gospels. One or two indeed of those miracles may seem, as Dr. Newman says, 'more or less improbable, being unequal in dignity to the rest'; and it has been suggested in consequence that they may be apocryphal. But Dr. Newman's own view is critically quite as reasonable, that 'they are supported by the system in which they are found, as being a few out of a multitude, and therefore but exceptions (and as we suppose but apparent exceptions) to the general rule.'   And with these questionable exceptions, there is a dignity, a beauty, a reserve of power, a restriction of use, a depth of spiritual significance, in the miracles attributed to Christ, which makes us feel that they are not merely congruous with His whole personality, but part of it. We cannot separate the wonderful life, or the wonderful teaching, from the wonderful works. They involve and interpenetrate, and presuppose each other, and form in their indissoluble combination one harmonious picture.   But that picture, to repeat once more the old but unanswerable dilemma, cannot by any ingenuity be construed into the mere likeness of a man ; while it is the most adequate portrait that imagination can conceive of an Incarnate God.   It is not indeed the kind of Incarnation that if left to ourselves we should have invented ; but for that very reason it is the kind that must be true.

This, then, was the original evidence on which the Incarnation was received.   It was the gradual self-revelation of a Person to spiritually minded persons.   But among the attributes of this Person was included the power of working miracles; and there cannot be a shadow of doubt that this was an integral element in the total impression which He produced.   His miracles did not prove His character, but they essentially confirmed the claim which His character meanwhile predisposed men to accept.

Now it is obvious that these miracles cannot appeal with such force to us, as they once did to contemporary eyes. But the very same lapse of time, which has diminished their effect, has increased that of another kind of evidence. For every successive century, that weakens the weight of bygone miracle, intensifies the wonder of bygone prophecy. And the Gospels are full of prophecy. Jesus Christ speaks with an absolute authoritative certainty of the everlasting nature of the kingdom which He came to found. 'The gates of hell shall not prevail against it'; 'Heaven and earth shall pass away, but My words shall not pass away'; and 'Lo, I am with you always, even unto the end of the world.' These and similar utterances are only indicative of His entire attitude towards the remote future. He speaks of it with unconditional certitude throughout. He is come to inaugurate a change within the souls of men which shall continue to operate till the end of time. When we remember to whom this promise was originally made—a few Jewish fishermen against the world, and those but half understanding their Master—the boldness of its prophecy is apparent. Yet its boldness is only equalled by its truth. For after overcoming the world for nineteen centuries, in the precise way that He foretold, the power of Christ is as strong as ever upon earth to-day. This then is our modern equivalent for the signs and wonders of an earlier age. The same unique Person confronts us with the same question as of old: 'Which of you convinceth Me of sin?' and 'If I speak truth, why do ye not believe Me?' But the words have a new significance; for included in their scope are nineteen centuries of prophecy fulfilled. We cannot regard the miracles of Christ therefore as merely things of long ago; for they are integral parts of a living system which confronts the world to-day, and vindicates its wondrous origin, by the actual fact of its present wonder.

Moreover, it must be remembered that, in our Christian view, the Incarnation was redemptive. It was an atonement. Sin, or moral evil, is a part of our total human experience, which philosophy is bound to take into account; and sin, though primarily due to the will, has infected the bodily organism of the whole human race; moral and physical depravity mingling with, and reacting on each other, till the entire resultant may be spoken of as 'the body of this death'—a complex whole in which it is impossible to disentangle the spiritual element from the diseased conditions and perverted functions of organ and tissue, which personal and ancestral sins have brought about.

And this amounts to saying, that there is one department of the world in which demonstrably

the reign of law breaks down.   The motions of the
stars are mathematically accurate ; vegetable life
pursues its annual round ; animals, till man has
touched them, follow the instincts of their kind.
But with man the case is different.   His appetites
and instincts are as well adapted as those of other
animals to ensure the preservation of the individual
and the race, yet he continually misuses them to
the detriment of both.   His reason endows him
with an unique capacity for promoting the progress
of his kind, yet his almost habitual use of it is self-
regarding and anti-social.   His will is conscious of
a moral law, yet disobeys it.   His whole body and
soul are involved in one complex, composite disease,
due to the violation of the appropriate and natural
laws of his species.   This condition therefore is
quite accurately described in the New Testament
as lawlessness (ἀνομία), and involves a real breach
of universal order—a miracle in the objectionable
sense of the term.   And it cannot be too often
repeated that this condition of humanity is no
philosophical hypothesis, or theological dogma, but
a perfectly familiar fact of our daily experience ;
—an experience which is apt, indeed, to be over-
looked in our more ordinary moments, simply
because it is so habitual, but which from time to
time arrests us with an intensity of awfulness
which language has no power to express.   It is at
once as certain as, and more stupendous than, any

other fact that we know. Now a primary object
of the Incarnation, as Christians believe, was to
remedy this lawlessness, to restore this inordinate
state of humanity to order. And historically this
has been its effect. Real Christians in every age
have both experienced and exhibited the gradual
restitution of their entire personality to order. The
work of Jesus Christ therefore comes before us, not
as an hypothetical breach of nature's laws, but as
the actual restitution of these laws when obviously,
and beyond controversy, broken—the counteraction
of the ' miracle ' of sin.

Now this consideration does not of course affect
the physical possibility of what are commonly
called miracles, which is a thing that few sane
men would deny. But it profoundly affects the
a priori probability of their occurrence, which is
really the point at issue in most arguments upon
the subject. For, instead of asking, ' Is God likely
to interfere with His own laws?' we should ask,
' Is He not likely to restore them when already
interfered with?' The interference is a fact; it is
daily before our eyes; its appalling consequences
are within us, and around us. Yet it is an anomaly
in the universe, and the more we learn of the
otherwise harmonious order of that universe, the
more irresistibly we feel that such a fact cannot
be final; and thus the likelihood of God's intervention assumes the highest possible probability.

But if such a counteraction of sin is to be brought about, it must be by the production, in one way or another, of a sinless humanity; which would be in harmony with the order of the universe. While in proportion as human beings are out of harmony with the order of the universe, a sinless person would not only appear, but be, from the human point of view, miraculous. We should have no standard with which to compare Him, and therefore no capacity to criticize either the conditions of His existence, or the range of His powers.

Now all this has an important bearing upon the miracles recorded in the Gospels. First and foremost among these miracles stands the virgin birth of Christ. And the real ground on which it is rejected is the *a priori* one of its intrinsic improbability. For the various mythological and critical considerations which are adduced against it are all dependent upon and subsidiary to this. But in the light of what we have been saying, is it intrinsically improbable? The tradition of the early Church was that only so could the sinful entail be broken off; and that at a time when the relation of soul and body was conceived as far less intimate than we now know it to be. But with our modern knowledge of their mutual interdependence, it is doubly impossible to conceive that natural human generation should issue in anything else than a contaminated personality. It may be urged that we have no reason to think otherwise, even in the case of a virgin birth. But the cases are widely different. For of natural generation we have positive knowledge, based on universal experience, that it does as a fact issue in a sinful person. Whereas of virgin birth we have no positive knowledge; it is wholly outside our experience; we can only conjecture what its consequence would be. And in the absence of all knowledge, it is a perfectly conceivable conjecture, that a mode of birth from which an essential factor of ordinary heredity is absent, should involve independence from hereditary taint.

When, therefore, we find a virgin birth asserted in Christian history and tradition, there can be no possible probability against it. Given ordinary human nature alone, it would be impossible; but given an Incarnation, whose object was to introduce a sinless personality into the world—to which an immaculate body is as essential as an uncontaminated soul—its congruity, and therefore its probability, are obvious. In a word, it can only be rejected on *a priori* grounds; and these grounds rest on the assumption that sinful humanity is normal; but once recognize that it is abnormal, an anomaly in the universe; *a priori* objections vanish and historic tradition resumes its sway. A complete break with sinful heredity is of the very essence of the Incarnation: and the account of the method of that breach which has come down to us, rests on precisely the same evidence as our account of the Incarnation itself.

Then there are the miracles of healing which occupy so prominent a place in the Gospels. These seem to many minds more credible, as being conceivably capable of naturalistic explanation. But it should be noticed that, however far such conjectural explanation may carry us, it does not reach the root of the matter. Christ emphasizes the connexion between sin and disease, as two aspects of one disordered personality; and connects His healing of the one with His forgiving of the other, as parts of the same redemptive work. He does not appear as the mere pitiful physician of exceptional ability; but as having power on earth to forgive sins, and therefore to remedy their physical effects. He claims to have come to destroy the dominion of evil in the world, by striking once for ever at its spiritual root; and as the sin of the soul has grown incorporate in the flesh, He heals diseases, not only in mercy, but in actual manifestation of the change which He is come to effect in the entire personality of man. In other words, while Christ's acts of physical healing are quite subordinate to His spiritual teaching, and are treated by Him as such, yet they are not merely incidental acts of mercy; they are an integral part of His entire work, an essential element in the total impression which He plainly designed to create, that He was Lord of the material as well as of the spiritual order, and came not merely to teach, but to exercise absolute authority over the bodies as well as the souls of men.

The same principle underlies what may be called the cosmic miracles, those, that is, which more obviously imply power over the general processes of the material universe; with which should be classed the raising of the dead. These evince superhuman power, but power which moves along rational lines, and is controlled. Christ sternly refuses to work them for a personal end, or to gratify a faithless curiosity which they would not convince. They have always some tender, merciful, spiritual purpose; and the momentary marvel is carefully linked again to the customary course of nature, in a way to suggest that it is nowise intended to supersede ordinary law. Food is multiplied, but its fragments are immediately ordered to be economized. The dead are raised, but their friends are bidden to feed them, and release them from the cerements of the grave. There is to be no unpractical lingering in a world of wonder: human life must at once resume its course. And the total picture is not of one who recklessly worked wonders, such as ignorant ages have loved to attribute to their heroes; but of one who, possessing superhuman power, only employed it with extreme reserve; to manifest and symbolize the superhuman character of His personality and work.

Finally, there is the crowning miracle of the Resurrection, on which the early Church laid so much stress.   It is easy enough to say that the continued existence of Jesus Christ, and not His corporeal Resurrection, is the important thing to believe.   But this ignores the previous question, 'Who and What was Jesus Christ? Did He, in the way that we have stated, connect disease and death with sin, and control material things at His will? Was His absolute supremacy over death as well as sin an integral part of the claim which He made, and which He promised to substantiate? and is matter an essential element in human personality as we know it?'   If so, whence comes the presumption that He either could not, or would not, re-assume His immaculate body, and indefinitely extend its powers? Simply from the fact that all other human bodies decay in the grave, and are turned again to their earth.   But all other human bodies are intimately contaminated by sin, whereas Christ's is, *ex hypothesi*, immaculate ; and while we know that throughout life the soul moulds and modifies the body, we have no means whatever of knowing what the nature or extent of this modification would be, when induced, not only by a sinless soul, but by a divine personality, on a sinless body. We cannot conceive that anything short of dissolution should eradicate the taint from the sinful body. It must be unmade if it is to be remade at all. But a sinless body, moulded by a sinless soul, is in no such case ; and we have no reason whatever to suppose that it might not be resumed at will: while such a resumption would be the appropriate—the obviously appropriate—climax to the whole of Christ's previous attitude towards matter ; the final manifestation of His personal triumph over the totality of sin—its consequence as well as its cause —and thus the earnest of His power to restore man's entire personality to ultimate order.

CHAPTER V

THE INCARNATION AND MIRACLES

WE have urged, in the last chapter, in general defence of the Christian tradition, that the miracles recorded in the Gospels are not merely inseparable from their context, but also profoundly harmonious with our conception of the Incarnation as a whole. But there is a class of thinkers in the present day who tend, in some sense, to believe the Incarnation, and yet to disbelieve in miracles; and who would therefore substitute for the Christian tradition a non-miraculous Christianity, as being more in accordance with the spirit of the age. Now it must be remembered that the opposition to miracles is as old as Christian history, and has passed through many phases which the Christian creed has outlived and survived. And this naturally leads us to ask whether its present phase is really final; or only one more wave of negative opinion whose strength is already beginning to be spent? The modern form of objection to miracles comes chiefly, of course, from Spinoza and Hume, than whom it has never found, nor is ever likely to find, abler exponents. But its particular revival in the present day would seem, especially, to date from the time when 'uniformity' became the dominant category of thought; when logic was being based upon the 'law of uniformity'; when uniformitarianism was overpressed in geology; and natural selection was allowed, in consequence, unlimited millions of ages for its action; with the general result that present phenomena were too readily assumed to be adequate criteria of the past. And at a time like this, when the popular logicians laid stress on the uniformity of nature, and yet admitted that this so-called law could in no way be proved, but must be 'begged,' Dr. Mozley defended miracles by accepting this position, and showing that we could give no reason whatever for our belief in the order of nature; and consequently that an interference with that order could not be called irrational; it might conflict with our expectation, but not with our reason. And this was a valid *argumentum ad hominem*; a valid answer to any rejection of miracles, drawn from the uniformity of nature. But that phrase, of shallow meaning and questionable value (seeing that no two things in nature were ever exactly alike), has now, to a great extent, lost its vogue. There was an undue simplicity about it, which has been considerably modified by the subsequent progress of science.

For our increase of scientific knowledge has also
increased our scientific agnosticism, by widening
the horizon of what remains to be known; and
men are becoming far more ready to recognize that
'there are more things in heaven and earth than
are dreamed of in our philosophy.' And we now
think less of the uniformity than of the unity of
nature; that unity which the very word 'universe'
implies; the intimate correlation between the whole
and its parts, between the parts and their whole;
which Tennyson's 'flower in the crannied wall' is so
often quoted to illustrate :—

> 'Little flower—but if I could understand
> What you are, root and all, and all in all,
> I should know what God and man is.'

At first sight this conception may seem to make
the difficulty of miracles become graver, since it
increases the magnitude of the 'interference' or
'alteration' which they involve. But this is not
in reality its ultimate effect. For uniformity may
be merely mechanical; but unity is essentially a
spiritual conception. 'The ego is the only unity,'
says Royard Collier, 'that is given us immediately
by nature. We do not meet with unity in sensible
experience, but the mind finds it within itself, and
thence transfers it to the outer world by analogy.'
We can easily see that this is so : for if, by an effort
of abstraction, we separate the material element in

experience from the spiritual, what is it that we find: a succession of passing phenomena, external to each other; whose every fresh phase and moment obliterates the last; like the waves upon a torrent, or the transformations of a dream; a world of which the old sceptical dictum would be true, πάντα ῥεῖ καὶ οὐδὲν μένει, 'all things are in perpetual flux, and there is no permanence at all.' In actual life, however, we do not make this abstraction; but habitually and instinctively read our own spiritual unity into the manifold variety of things. We connect and correlate the various impressions of our senses, things as different as scent and sound and touch; we look before and after, and link the present to the past,—the past which would otherwise have ceased to be; we gather and group and compare, within the mirror of our mind, the scattered phenomena of distant space; we weave out of what by themselves would be disconnected, incoherent elements, an unity, a system, a whole. But in so doing we are not creating but only recreating for ourselves, a world which already exists without us. That world is not a chaotic flux, as it would be if merely material, but an orderly system of things. Atoms combine in mathematical proportion; stars move in their courses by mechanical rule; organic life in plant and animal is minutely, elaborately teleological; man is guided and developed by a moral law.

And the result is a coherent universe whose elements are intimately bound together, by the mutual
ministrations of all to each and each to all.   But
all these links are obviously spiritual; and analogous to what we find within ourselves.   And thus
the unity of nature must be due to the action of
a spiritual power.   The phrase indeed has no other
meaning; for we cannot conceive a merely material
unity; since spirit is the only unifying agent that
we know.   Thus the more science impresses upon
us the unity of nature, the more does it, by implication, assert that nature is rooted and grounded in
spirit.   Now spirit, as we have repeatedly seen,
affirms the absolute supremacy of its own ends.
It claims as of right to govern, and never to
subserve matter; to use matter for spiritual purposes, and never the reverse.   And whenever the
reverse takes place, and we see spiritual beings
using their powers in pursuit of animal, and therefore material ends, we recognize at once that they
are contradicting the very essence of their nature,
and are therefore unrighteous or wrong.

If then the whole of nature is rooted and grounded
in spirit, and the primary characteristic of spirit is
this absolute self-assertion, the antecedent probability of miracles is immensely increased.   In the
days of deism, when nature was regarded as a
machine set going once for all, interference with
its regularity may well have seemed impossible;

and the exaggerated estimate of the uniformity of nature was largely a legacy from those days. But if nature is only sustained by its intimate union with spirit, and spirit is what we have above described, it is no wonder that the processes of nature should be modified for an adequate spiritual end.

It was moreover more or less implied in the older objection to miracles, that we had a complete knowledge of the processes of nature ; and could therefore see that there was no room, so to speak, for the miraculous element to intervene. But the more we recognize that nature has always a spiritual coefficient, the less confident does this assurance become. For in this case all causation, however mechanical upon the surface, must obviously run back into the spiritual region, or in other words be ultimately spiritual. This indeed is a conviction which has been gaining ground ever since Hume's analysis of causation. We have come to see with increasing clearness that physical causes are not causes at all, in the sense which our reason or causal instinct demands. They are only antecedents or conditions that transmit causation which they cannot themselves originate.

For our whole notion of cause is confessedly derived from what takes place within ourselves. As self-conscious beings we can be also self-determined ; we can frame our own ideals, fashion our own plans, choose which, of many suggested motives,

we will make our own; and all this without any
compulsion from without.   We can then realize
our ideals, prosecute our plans, pursue our purpose
in the outer world; and in so doing, initiate events
of which our own will is the veritable starting-
point, since it includes both their 'how' and their
'why,' is at once both their origin and explanation.
Thus our will is an agent whose reason for action is
contained within itself, and as such a self-explana-
tory agent.   When we have traced an occurrence to
the intervention of the human will, we are at once
content.   It is fully accounted for.   We know not
merely how it began, but why, (its *raison d'être*)
and have therefore reached its absolute beginning.
This then is the source of our conception of cause,
and this is what we mean by the term :—something
which initiates changes without external compulsion, and therefore out of its own inner nature, and
is hence their real starting-point; a self-determined
and therefore self-conscious, and therefore spiritual
being.   And this is what we postulate in the universe at large, when we say that it must have a
cause.   It must originate in a will which is its own
law, and therefore its own explanation (*caussa sui*),
or, in mediaeval phrase, a being whose will and
intellect are one.

And it is only in the light of this postulate that
we can talk of secondary or natural causes.   They
are parts of a caused whole which in their context

partake of the causality of that whole, and therefore
of its ultimate spirituality; but by themselves they
are not causes at all, but merely media for trans-
mission of causation. 'We never exhaust the whole
mass of conditions,' says a modern logician, 'which
produce the effect. The event never comes, and it
never could come, from the abstract selection which
we call the cause. We imply the presence of
unspecified conditions, but since these are normal
we omit to mention them [1].' And foremost among
those conditions is the vital connexion of the universe at every moment with its first cause; for this,
as we have seen, is what its unity implies. He
sustains it in being; and the mechanical laws, on
which what we commonly call natural causation
depends, are, as Lotze says, not 'laws which the
divine action "*obeys*," but which it really at each
moment creates.' 'For they could not have
existed prior to God as a code to which He accom-
modated Himself; they can only be the expression
to us of the mode in which He works.'

'And though He thunder by law, the law is still
     His voice [2].'

Hume's negative criticism of causation was, as
we said, the involuntary means of turning thought
into the above direction. For it was impossible to
rest content with his sceptical conclusions, which

[1] Bradley, *Logic*.   [2] Tennyson, *Higher Pantheism*.

would have made science and philosophy alike
impossible; and in the process of meeting them,
Kant and others came to recognize the fact that
the causal nexus is ultimately spiritual.   But Malebranche, long before Hume, had expressed both
sides of the case with admirable clearness.   'Les
causes *naturelles*,' he says, 'ne sont point de véri-
tables causes, ce ne sont que des causes *occasionnelles*,
qui n'agissent que par la force et l'efficace de la
volonté de Dieu[1].'

But if the action of natural causes is thus dependent on divine concurrence, or is in other words
an aspect of the divine energy at work, our previous
conclusion is further fortified.   For so far from
knowing the whole of any physical process, it is
obvious that we only know a part—the appearance
in fact or part that meets the eye: while the
spiritual power which from moment to moment
produces natural phenomena, may be reasonably
conceived to change them, on occasion, for an
adequate end.   We shall not need therefore at the
present day to use Mozley's *argumentum ad hominem*—that belief in the uniformity of nature is an
irrational impulse—except with those who are still
slaves to that uniformity.   On the contrary, we
recognize that the unity of nature, and the causal
connexion of its parts, is a rational conviction, but
one which inevitably lands us in the spiritual region;

---

[1] Malebranche, *De la Methode*, vi. ii. 3.

and therefore makes it easy to believe that the
spirit which habitually controls matter, may sometimes exhibit its supremacy in extraordinary ways.
Human analogy—and it is the highest we have—is
entirely in favour of this.   For the greater a man
is, the more methodical and consistent he will be in
all the usual situations of life ; one whose conduct
can be calculated, and whose character relied on.
But, in a crisis, the same greatness will be shown
by ability to extemporize and courage to innovate ;
while lesser men are paralyzed by slavish adher-
ence to routine.   The great man does not contradict himself, but, for a new purpose, calls new
powers into play, and at the next moment is as
regular, as orderly, as punctual as ever : the fact that
he has habits does not alter the fact that he is free.
So the habitual course of nature, which alone makes
life and knowledge possible, may well be traversed
by lightning flashes from the spiritual world, if both
alike are being guided by one power to one end,
and that end, in the strict sense, supernatural.

Hence it is obvious that the probability of
miracles cannot be settled by a rough and ready
appeal to experience, but depends upon the kind
of experience which we include under the term ; or
in other words upon the presuppositions with which
we approach experience.   This is forcibly expressed
by Dr. Newman, in a passage which may be worth
quoting, from his *Essay on Miracles*.

'When the various antecedent objections which ingenious men have urged against miracles are brought together, they will be found nearly all to arise from forgetfulness of the existence of moral laws. In their zeal to perfect the laws of matter they most unphilosophically overlook a more sublime system, which contains disclosures not only of the Being, but of the Will of God. Thus, Hume observes, " Though the Being to whom the miracle is ascribed be Almighty, it does not, upon that account, become a whit more probable, since it is impossible for us to know the attributes or actions of such a Being, otherwise than from the experience which we have of His productions in the usual course of nature. This still reduces us to past observation, and obliges us to compare the instances of the violation of truth in the testimony of men with those of the violation of the laws of nature by miracles, in order to judge which of them is most likely and probable." The moral government of God, with the course of which the miracle entirely accords, is altogether kept out of sight . . . And a recent author adopts a similarly partial and inconclusive mode of reasoning, when he confuses the Christian miracles with fables of apparitions and witches, and would examine them on the strict principle of those legal forms which from their secular object go far to exclude all religious discussion of the question. Such reasoners seem to suppose, that when the agency of the Deity is introduced to account for miracles, it is the illogical introduction of an unknown cause, a reference to a mere name, the offspring, perhaps, of popular superstition; or, if more than a name, to a cause that can be known only by means of the physical creation; and hence they consider religion as founded in the mere weakness or eccentricity of the intellect, not in actual intimations of a divine government as contained in the moral world[1].'

What this means is not that the moral and material order are in any contrast or contradiction; they are obviously and incontestably part and parcel of one and the self-same system. But whereas we know that system, in its material aspect, only from without—its surface, so to speak, and perhaps an inch or two below; there is one point at which we penetrate within it, and feel that we are nearer to the heart of things; and that is our personal experience of our own internal state—

'I myself am what I know not—ignorance
        which proves no bar
To the knowledge that I am, and, since I am,
        can recognize
What to me is pain and pleasure; this is sure,
        the rest—surmise[2].

[1] Newman, *Essay on Miracles*, § 2, p. 20.
[2] Browning, *La Saisiaz*.

.   .   .   .

Mere surmise: my own experience—that is
knowledge, once again[1]!'

And at the very root of this personal experience,
which is our only first-hand knowledge, we find the
moral law, with its imperious claim to subordinate
all things to itself.   Thus what I know to be at
once the most certain, and the most fundamental
fact of experience is the moral law with its claim to
supremacy.   There is nothing irrational, therefore,
in believing that, on occasion, in deference to that
claim, the material order may give way to the
moral, and

'Miracle was duly wrought
When, save for it, no faith was possible.
Whether a change were wrought i' the shows
     o' the world,
Whether the change came from our minds
     which see
Of the shows o' the world so much as and no
     more
Than God wills for His purpose[2].'

This then is, in brief, our position.   We fully
grant that nature is uniform, in the sense that
similar causes, under similar conditions, will always
produce similar effects; but we entirely deny that

[1] Browning, *La Saisiaz.*
[2] Id. *A Death in the Desert.*

I

this principle justifies the assertion that what does not happen to-day cannot ever have happened: firstly, because we never know all the conditions even of what is happening to-day, and much less of what was happening centuries ago; secondly, because among those conditions is the presence of the spiritual power, on which their existence and operation depends; and which as spiritual, and therefore rational and free, can initiate a change at any point—a change not against nature, but against our ordinary experience of nature,—*non contra naturam sed contra quam est nota natura*, as Augustine well expressed it long ago.

On this presence and operation of the absolute spirit in all cases of causation Lotze has some remarks, which are precisely to our point :—

'We are not,' he says, 'to picture the absolute, placed in some remote region of extended space, and separated from the world of its creations, so that its influence has to retraverse a distance and make a journey in order to reach things; for its indivisible unity, omnipresent at every point, would fill this space as well as others. . . . Wherever in apparent space an organic germ has been formed, at that very spot and not removed from it the absolute is present. Nor . . . is it simply this class of facts which compels us to assume such an action of the absolute. We may regard the process by which

things that possess a life and soul are formed as
something unusual and superior ; but the presence
of the absolute which makes this process possible
is no less the basis necessarily implied in the most
insignificant interaction of any two atoms. Nor
again do we think of its presence as a mere uniform
breath which penetrates all places, and this particular spot among them, like that subtle, formless,
and homogeneous ether from which many strange
theories expect the vivification of matter into the
most various forms ; but the absolute is indivisibly
present with the whole inner wealth of its nature
in this particular spot, and in obedience to those
laws of its action which it has itself laid down,
necessarily makes additions to the simple conjunctions of those elements which are themselves only
its own continuous actions, simple additions where
the conjunctions are simple, additions of greater
magnitude and value where they are more compli-
cated. Everywhere it draws only the consequences,
which at every point of the whole belong to the
premisses it has previously realized at that point [1].'

Now the Incarnation, in our Christian view of it,
is a supreme instance of this action of the Absolute ;
the Being who is behind all things therein coming
to their front, and exhibiting as a necessary part
of the process His authoritative relation to the

[1] Lotze, *Metaphysic*, § 246.

world.   We believe it primarily for a combination of moral and spiritual reasons, but once believed it affects our whole view of the material universe. For it has a cosmic, as well as a human significance. It is not merely an event in the history of man, but an event, at least as far as our earth is concerned, in the history of matter ; analogous upon a higher plane to the origin of life, or the origin of personality ; the appearance of a new order of being in the world.   And precisely as, in Browning's language,

'Man, once descried, imprints for ever
His presence on all lifeless things[1],'
so

'the acknowledgement of God in Christ
Accepted by thy reason, solves for thee
All questions in the earth and out of it[2].'

That is to say, it must for all who believe it become the absolutely central truth of their philosophy.   Just as the Copernican astronomy, or the doctrine of evolution, have enlarged and modified our views of the universe, so the Incarnation, once accepted, throws a new light upon the entire world. For on the one hand, against mere idealism, it emphasizes the value and importance of matter, as being the agent through which God's spiritual purpose is effected : and on the other hand, against mere materialism, it interprets this value and im-

[1] Browning, *Paracelsus.*   [2] Id. *A Death in the Desert.*

portance, as consisting in the capability to subserve that purpose. Thus while rejecting the respective negations of idealism and materialism, it sanctions their positive elements—the supremacy of spirit and the reality of matter; and so supplementing each by the other, combines both in a concrete whole.

This view of the Incarnation is sometimes, ignorantly, regarded as if it were only an ingenious afterthought of modern apology. But that is merely because it sank into comparative abeyance, in the eighteenth century, when men were more occupied with negative criticism than with positive systems of thought. As a matter of fact it is as old as Christianity: it is latent, not to say patent, in the prologue of St. John, and the Epistles of St. Paul: it has been proclaimed by Christian philosophers, in every philosophic age: and, with the revival of constructive thinking, it has of necessity revived.

To object that revealed truths can have no speculative value, and that philosophy cannot take account of revelation, as such, is to under-estimate the range of philosophy. For philosophy must deal with the totality of knowledge. It contemplates in Plato's phrase 'all time and all existence.' It cannot, without self-destruction, ignore any kind of fact. But if there has been a revelation, it must have brought new facts—and those important ones —to our knowledge; and once within the field of knowledge, they are of necessity within the field of philosophy. Thenceforth, to philosophize without them is not merely to leave them open questions, but implicitly to rule them out of court as being untrue; while to philosophize with them is to be modified by them, in the way and degree that we have described—to make the Incarnation the centre of our speculation, as well as of our practical life; the light of our thoughts, as well as the guide of our acts.

But even so, it is sometimes asked, can we not conceive an Incarnation without miracles; and might not such a conception be equally the centre of a yet very different view of the world?

Undoubtedly; within limits we might frame such a conception. But we do not believe in the Incarnation because we can conceive it, but because we have a conviction that it happened. And the only evidence we have that it happened, is also evidence that it happened in a certain way. To borrow from that evidence the general notion of an Incarnation, and then proceed to clothe it in the colours of our own imagination, is absurd. And the only alternative is to accept the miraculous accompaniment of the Incarnation as we find it, and, so doing, to view the world in its light.

There is one further question to which these considerations inevitably lead.

Why do not miracles happen now? If the

power of Christ on earth is as real now as in the first century, why should it not be accompanied by similar results? Does not the absence of miracle now, from the only Christian life that we can really test, go far to disprove its presence in the past? Now this question, though it is often asked, and constitutes a real difficulty to many minds, tacitly assumes that in accepting the miracles of Christ, we accept the position that Christianity was meant to be a miraculous religion. Whereas the precise converse is the case. We regard the miracles of Christ as unique manifestations of His unique personality: things which indeed we could not have foreseen, but which we recognize, when once recorded, as eminently congruous with His life and work. He claimed to be superhuman, and the claim required substantiation to gain a hearing. Attention had to be arrested; expectation had to be aroused; the advent of a new era had to be emphasized; and that in an age, and among a people that was ready to accept miracles, and therefore to whom miracles were a natural—not to say inevitable—mode of address. Authority, absolute, unqualified, paramount authority, is the essential characteristic of the life of Christ; and that authority must needs be exhibited, in order to be received. It is difficult even to conceive how otherwise a beginning could have been made.

But the very fact that the miracles of Christ

seem, from this point of view, so natural, makes it all the more instructive to notice the severe economy with which they are used. He never once employs them to relieve His personal necessities, but lives and suffers in strict obedience to the ordinary laws of nature. He refuses to work them to confute enemies, and warns His disciples that after all they are subordinate things. He carefully connects them, as we have noticed above, with the customary course of life, in a way to show that they were not meant to supersede it :—e. g. 'Go shew thyself to the priest.'—'Go wash in Siloam.'—'Gather up the fragments that remain.'—'He commanded that something should be given her to eat.'—'Loose him, and let him go.' There is no sign in all this of any intention to introduce a reign of miracle, bringing intellectual confusion into the world. On the contrary, the fact that Christ manifestly could, yet habitually would not overrule it, gives additional emphasis to the reign of law—an emphasis which the whole tenor of His teaching serves further to enforce. For the burden of that teaching is that the course of nature is the will of God, and that faith should recognize that will everywhere : in the clothing of the lilies, the feeding of the ravens, the fall of a sparrow, the sunshine and the rain ; not less than in the sicknesses that punish, or the catastrophes that execute swift judgement upon sin. Christian life accordingly consists in accepting the order of events, not in the spirit of fatalism, but in the spirit of faith; not expecting to be exempt from what is common to man, but, patiently enduring to the end, 'as seeing Him that is invisible.' This recognition of spiritual significance, where the bodily eye sees none, is the very essence of the Christian probation; the characteristic distinction of the Christian life. It is that walking by faith and not by sight, that belief of those who have not seen, upon which the Gospels and Epistles alike lay all their stress. And to make this possible, miracles, in the ordinary sense, must cease. But they cease, it should be noticed, as the scattered lights of sunrise fade into the fullness of an ampler day. They cease because the fact which they sporadically emphasized has now become a Christian commonplace; the fact that divine providence everywhere and always uses matter for the furtherance of spiritual ends. They do not vanish out of history as though they had never been, and leave man to lapse into apathetic acceptance of the inexorable order of events. They have inaugurated a new epoch: they have interpreted the order of events afresh: they have accentuated and intensified the providential aspect of the world. And their perpetual trace remains in the abiding consciousness of Christians that 'all things work together for good to them that love God.'

The cessation therefore of miracles was as needful

as their occurrence: and we no longer look to meet with them in ordinary life. But they have irradiated the world for us, and left a glow behind them which is still 'the master light of all our seeing.' For they have led us to face nature not with passive resignation, but with active faith,—faith which not only reads in its general aspect a revelation of God, but often also in its particular incidents a mission and a message to individual men. Such faith cannot of course be tested by the methods of a laboratory or a law-court; and is too private and peculiar even to be publicly proclaimed. But there is no question that it is a normal element of spiritual experience with which Christians have been familiar in every age; the conviction that outward events have at times been so appositely ordered in relation to their personal needs, as to prove beyond power of doubting that the processes of nature are, at least on occasion, utilized in the interest of man. This is a belief, which it is obvious, cannot be produced in argument; though at the same time it profoundly affects the Christian attitude towards argument; by endowing its possessors with a certitude which no critical attack can shake. '*At ubi sunt illi depicti...*' may be quoted against it in vain. Though therefore it cannot be used in argument, the fact of its widespread existence should have weight. For it is no mere sentimental fancy, or superstition of the ignorant and foolish. It has

been shared by the wise and practical, the men of
ideas, and the men of affairs. In every age and
nation, Christians of every sort and kind have
believed themselves in contact with a living, personal,
particular providence, working through material as
well as spiritual means. They have felt that, in
answer to prayer, or at critical moments in their
life, outward events have aroused and controlled
them, as distinctly as a voice or hand; things which
often at the time seemed merely natural phenomena,
yet afterwards were recognized as ministers of God.

> 'I can but testify
> God's care for me—no more, can I—
> It is but for myself I know;
>
> .   .   .   .
>
> No mere mote's-breadth but teems immense
> With witnessings of providence :
>
> .   .   .   .
>
> Have I been sure, this Christmas-Eve,
> God's own hand did the rainbow weave,
> Whereby the truth from heaven slid
> Into my soul? I cannot bid
> The world admit He stooped to heal
> My soul, as if in a thunder-peal
> Where one heard noise, and one saw flame,
> I only knew He named my name[1].'

This belief in a special providence is not the
same as a belief in miracles; but it rests on a very

[1] Browning, *Christmas Eve.*

similar view of the world. For it implies that the
souls of men, in their separate history and destiny,
are objects of peculiar, personal interest to God:
while nature — material nature — that seems so
changeless in its course, is yet an instrument, when
rightly viewed, through which that interest is
shown. Now though these thoughts had often
risen in men's minds before, there can be no
question that they received a novel and final
emphasis from Jesus Christ. He first taught men
to regard the world, as children look upon their
father's house, with a secure sense in it, of being
everywhere at home. And it is an old remark
that even physical science owes more than we often
think, to the friendly attitude towards nature which
this teaching introduced. But miracles were among
the means, as we have seen cause to believe, which
Christ employed to give weight to His words:
leading men to trust His interpretation of the world
by visible proof that the world was His own. If
then our intimate faith in providence comes to us
from Christ, it is lineally connected with the
wonders that He wrought. For it is the inner
reality, the essential truth, which those wonders
were used to enforce, in an age and among a race
where it could only have gained credence by their
means. And now, in its turn, it makes them
credible, by the ever-recurring experience of its own
intrinsic wonder.

CHAPTER VI

THE INCARNATION AND SACRAMENTS

WE have seen that the aspect of the material universe has a profound religious influence on man; but matter has another kind of connexion with religion, which is hardly less important, arising from the reaction upon it of the human mind. A flower growing in the field, quick with form and scent and colour, is far fairer than one dried between the pages of a book; yet though the former may indeed give us 'thoughts that do often lie too deep for tears,' the latter may be linked with tender memories of bygone love, which invest it with greater power over our personal life. So beside the general religious impression which the beauty and wonder of the world creates, we find special associations of spiritual import gathered round particular material things; and matter has thus what may be called a secondary as well as a primary connexion with religion. Historically speaking, indeed, the former is even more prominent than the latter in the early stages of human

development. For the distinction in question closely
corresponds to that between myth, and ritual or
cultus, with which we are nowadays so familiar;
and of these, cultus in early religion so often over-
shadows myth, that it has even been supposed by
some to precede it. Thus myths embody what
may be called the primary teachings of nature, the
simple spiritual ideas which its aspect inevitably
awakes in the mind of man; while cultus depends
upon the various secondary associations, by which
man has invested particular places and actions and
things with spiritual significance, of a more or less
arbitrary kind.

Cultus then, in its widest sense, is concerned
with an immense variety of rites and things, of
very different degrees of dignity and worth. In
early religion, for example, there is the senseless
fetish; the sacred animal regarded as an ancestor
or god; the solemn feast at which the clans-
men renew their vital union by feeding together
the flesh, or life-blood, or emblem of their god;
on the various kinds of sacrifice which apparently
arose out of these communions; the sacred spots
which divers causes had invested with spiritual
awe; the ceremonial customs whereby life's epochs,
of birth, puberty, marriage, and death, were conse-
crated by the sanctions of religion. While when
we come to more civilized ages, and cultivated
races the same things reappear upon a higher level

of refinement. The rude idol gives place to the shapelier statue; the sacred grove or cave to the stately temple; the tribal communions to the solemn mysteries graced with art and song; cere-monies are multiplied, and sacrifices offered with grander pomp and circumstance. Nor did the progress of enlightenment as we may trace it in the various religious books of India, Persia, China, and Egypt, in any way diminish the importance of this material side of religion. It led to that clearer distinction between symbols and things symbol-ized, between external actions and internal motives, which attained its most complete expression in the Greek philosophers and Hebrew prophets. Yet even Plato, the great idealist, would have infinite attention bestowed upon the material conditions of spiritual culture; and Ezekiel, the especial prophet of personal responsibility, with all his insistence upon the immediate relation of the soul to God, reaffirms the elaborate ritual and symbolism of the Temple. Thus. throughout pre-Christian history, the phases of man's spiritual life are closely con-nected with material forms.

Now this connexion is often represented as simply and solely superstitious; especially since we have been enabled to trace its evolution from the primi-tive processes of savage thought, in which every-thing is animated, and material objects are naturally endowed with spiritual meaning, because they are

literally supposed to have souls of their own.   But
this misinterpretation of the principle of evolution,
as if it degraded all things to the level of their
earliest form of appearance, has again and again
been pointed out.   The true teaching of evolution
is that the higher form is implicitly contained in
the lower, and consequently that there is more
in the lower form than at first sight meets the eye.
And many of the instincts of primitive man were
truer than the explanations of them which he
attempted to give.   His judgements were better
than his reasons.   So in the present case : man is
progressive, and his religion has been the chief
factor in his progress.   No essential element of his
religion, therefore, can have been wholly irrational ;
and a very little reflection will suffice to show that
the connexion in question is an essential element in
his religion.   For spirit, as we have seen above, is
only known to human experience in combination
with matter, and primitive thought scarcely dis-
tinguishes the two.   When therefore a savage
believes in gods and spirits, who act upon him in
various ways, it is inevitable that he should localize
them in the supposed spheres of their activity : the
forest that thrills him ; the mountain top that awes
him ; the corn and wine that sustain his life ; or
the flash of lightning that may strike him dead.
This is no mere play of fancy, or irrational association of ideas : at a certain stage of culture it is

a psychological necessity, if divine presence and
divine action are to be realized at all.   And when
later on this crude localization gives place to sym-
bolic representation, the involved principle is the
same.   It is a far cry from the fetish to Athene of
the Parthenon ; but they both result from the like
inability to realize spirit apart from matter.

But the relation of gods to men is only one side
of religion ; there is also the relation of men to the
gods ; and this again, if it is to be real, must issue
in physical action.   Thus the partaking in the tribal
communion, the offering of sacrifice with its pre-
scribed ritual, the due performance of epochal
ceremonies, the observance of taboo, constitute the
practical religion of an early race.   Such things
may seem to us unspiritual, and so of course to
a great extent they were ; the external action
being all that was thought of, ἔθος ἄνευ φιλοσοφίας
as Plato calls it.   But they were the necessary
means by which spiritual life first came to recognize itself ; they called the will into play, and thus
actualized religion ; they kept ordinary life under
a control, which was ultimately spiritual, however
dimly understood as such, and which therefore contained the potency of all its subsequent development ; while for the higher minds they were the
inevitable stepping-stones to the higher forms of
conduct.   It is a mistake therefore to regard the
association of religious belief and practice with

material things as inevitably superstitious or irrational; for it is founded on a psychological necessity, from which there is no possibility of escape, in a world where spirit can only be realized through matter. Such association is of course a fruitful parent of superstition, when its underlying religion degenerates; but it is, nevertheless, the natural method by which religious progress has been made. Nor is it always possible, in a given case, to say where superstition began and progress ended, for the simple reason that we cannot replace ourselves either on the intellectual or moral level of the remote past.

Jacob's anointing of the stone at Bethel, where he dreamed of heaven, is an illustration of our point. It is a familiar instance of a custom once common the whole world over, and which has left its memorials in every land, degenerating at last into mere superstition. But in Jacob's case it is connected with a spiritual crisis in which a deeply religious character was deeply moved, and shows us how much reality may often underlie such customs. Indeed the Old Testament is full of instances to the point : ceremonies like circumcision, or the blood-anointing of the passover, or the dismissal of the scapegoat, are paralleled by modern anthropologists in every quarter of the globe : and can perhaps be traced to what are intellectually very crude conceptions, for their rise. But in the

Old Testament we see with what profound spiritual significance they were capable. of being invested, and of how much real religious development they may have been the vehicles ; and though these may be extreme cases, we may reasonably assume that similar feelings occurred elsewhere ; and that many a relic, which now only excites antiquarian interest in a museum, was once a spiritual symbol, an element in some soul's tragedy, charged with all the pathos of religious hopes and fears.

But the same line of thought will carry us further. The spiritual meaning, of which we have been speaking as connected with material things, is usually regarded as subjective and due to a more or less arbitrary association of ideas. But we have already had occasion to remark that the separation of subject and object is easier in language than in fact. The most intelligible sense which we have been able to give to 'reality' is permanent relation to a person or persons. If therefore a particular person realizes the divine presence, which we believe to be latent everywhere, with exceptional vividness in a particular place, does not this constitute an actual manifestation of God to that person in that place? For in what sense can it be said that God is not really present, when we apprehend His presence to such good purpose, that the whole of our subsequent conduct is coloured by the fact? The same could not of course be said of a being who was not omnipresent, or immanent throughout the universe.   But a Being who is omnipresent is, *vi termini*, present at all times and in all places.   When therefore He is recognized at a particular time or place, the recognition is not imaginary but real.   He is there and causes His own recognition, or reveals Himself.   So far indeed from God's universal immanence being incompatible with such particular presence, as is sometimes mistakenly supposed, it is the natural and necessary presupposition of it.   Because God is everywhere, He can appear anywhere; while because man is not everywhere, but limited to a particular time and place, his relation to God must be realized under the like particular conditions.

> 'Earth's crammed with heaven,
> And every common bush afire with God;
> But only he who sees takes off his shoes,
> The rest sit round it, and pluck blackberries,
> And daub their natural faces unaware
> More and more from the first similitude[1].'

Now if religion be true at all; if there be any such relation of God to man, as the human race has always, in one form or another, believed; this psychological necessity for its material expression is an additional argument for the Incarnation.   For the most perfect organ of material expression is

[1] E. B. Browning, *Aurora Leigh*.

confessedly the human body: and we cannot but
assume that if God really desires intercourse with
man, He will adopt its most perfect means.   And
thus again from this fresh point of view the Incarnation is antecedently probable : while, as we have said
in another context, once grant the probability, and
the life of Christ becomes its obvious fulfilment.

The life of Christ in the flesh then, as Christians
regard it, is the visible and tangible manifestation
('that which we have seen and our hands have
handled') of God's true relation to man, and man's
due relation to God.   It thus sanctions the instinctive tendency that we have traced in every stage of
culture, to realize this double relation by material
means ; and at the same time sublimates those
means to a power of spiritual expression which they
never possessed before.

In the first place the life of Christ shows us the
human body in a new light; shows us how that
body of flesh and blood, which even Plato called
a prison, may be the intimate ally as well as the
adequate organ of the soul.   For the body of
Christ was not merely the instrument of His
intercourse with men.   It was that, with its gracious
presence, its healing touch, its tears of sympathy,
its words and looks of love and warning, or of
righteous indignation.   But it was more than that ;
an integral element in His life and work.   He
controls its appetites under temptation; He goes

about when weary doing good; He foresees yet faces suffering; He masters pain to speak words of kindness; He accepts death by crucifixion. And these things do not merely show, they actually make His human character. The stress and strain of them fashions and forms it—matter thus contributing to shape the interior life which it also serves to express. And thus we see that the bodily organism, so far from being a hindrance, is an essential ingredient in the progressive development of holy personality.

Then there is Christ's attitude towards nature, and the external world: He declares that God is omnipresent in it. Heaven is God's throne and the earth is His footstool; and without Him not a sparrow falls on the ground. Consequently, we are to see in it the proof of God's care and love. 'Behold the fowls of the air . . . your heavenly Father feedeth them.' 'Consider the lilies of the field.' 'If God so clothe the grass of the field, shall He not much more clothe you?' 'He maketh His sun to rise upon the evil and the good, and sendeth rain upon the just and on the unjust.' Thus natural religion, as obviously flowing from the primary aspect of the material world, is the very starting-point and basis of Christ's teaching. But not less striking is His emphatic sanction of what we have called its secondary religious use, by the constant investiture of earthly objects with a spiritual significance.   Salt, light, wheat, tares, mustard-seed, leaven, pearls of price, the sheepfold, the vineyard, the harvest, the sunset, the lightning shining from the east unto the west, are all pressed into the service of the spirit.   Everywhere He 'touches things common till they rise to touch the spheres.'   And not only so, but He uses language that suggests a deep meaning for all this.   Earthly things symbolize spiritual, because they come from one author and are the expression of one mind, which repeats its creative phrases in a succession of ascending keys. Hence every lower foreshadows a higher in which its meaning is fulfilled, 'No chaffinch but implies the cherubim.'   Thus the clothing of the grass and the feeding of the ravens are prophetic of the clothing and feeding of man.   And the disciples are said to *be* the salt of the earth, the light of the world, labourers in the harvest, fishers of men; because they literally repeat the selfsame functions in a higher plane of existence; while finally Christ speaks of Himself not as resembling, but as being the veritable vine, the veritable bread, the veritable light of the world; implying that He is the absolute truth of all these things; the supreme reality which they partially manifest in their several spheres: the actual source of all material nutrition and illumination, as well as the spiritual life and light of men.

Nor does He only use symbolical language: His

life is full of symbolical action. He was baptized; He was anointed; He put forth His hand and touched the leper; He sighed and said Ephphatha; He spat and made clay and anointed the eyes of the blind; He stooped and wrote on the ground; He lifted up His eyes to heaven; He made a scourge of small cords; He washed His disciples' feet; He breathed on them; He lifted up His hands and blessed them. And He died by the only mode of death which could be visibly portrayed for ever, with all its profound appeal, to the eyes of men. Lastly, He ordained sacraments; selecting, as their media, the two simplest, most symbolical, most universal religious rites, the sacred ablution, and the sacred feast. Both these things were familiar to the world, as we have seen, and had their place under all kinds of religion. He raised and re-enacted them in their purest forms to be thenceforward means of union with Himself; and thus gave final recognition to the law we have traced by which matter is made ministrant to spiritual life.

Now when we review the life and teaching of Christ, we see at once upon what condition this ministry of matter takes place; what it is that makes it religious and not superstitious; progressive and not retrograde. The condition is that matter be always subordinate to spirit. We see this first in the bodily life. 'Man doth not live by bread alone'—'My meat is to do the will of Him that sent

Me'—that is the principle by which the body becomes a spiritual instrument. And in proportion as it is forgotten, and bodily appetite is viewed as an end instead of a means, the body ceases to be the spirit's organ, and becomes first its prison, and then its grave. The man loses his power of self-determination, the distinctive characteristic of spirit, and is inevitably determined from without; till he ends by becoming the mechanical automaton (the man machine) that materialism believes him always to be.

So with the parabolic teaching, there are those who see but do not perceive, because they cannot rise above the level of the letter which killeth— killeth, that is, if it is not risen above. While the forms of phrase which we have noticed above seem expressly designed to emphasize the supremacy of the spiritual element. I am, not I am like, the good shepherd, the door, the way, the vine; as though to say, I am the reality, before which the image sinks into unimportance; or again, the fields are ripe already to harvest, the real fields to the real harvest—and ye are, not ye are like, the salt of the earth, the light of the world. And in like manner in the matter of ordinances; 'the sabbath,' we are told, 'was made for man, not man for the sabbath.' 'It is the spirit that quickeneth, the flesh profiteth nothing.' 'The words that I speak unto you, they are spirit, and they are truth.'

Thus we see that the immemorial union of matter and spirit in religion was emphatically sanctioned by the practice and precept of Christ; while the complete subordination of the former to the latter was declared to be the condition of its legitimacy— the sole condition on which the functions of either could be duly fulfilled. And when we turn to Christian history we see the full effect of this.

In the first place there is the treatment of the human body;—that body which had so often previously been despised in theory and indulged in practice, that it had come to be the very enemy of the soul. Christianity changed all this. It swept away the sham contempt of the philosophers, and exalted the body to a position of unique dignity, by declaring it to be the temple of the Holy Ghost; while for the same reason It curbed its indulgence by showing that temperance and chastity are parts of the reverence due to so august a thing. It thus unified body and soul, as It unified the other elements of human personality; and all subsequent morality was coloured by the fact. The body lost its false independence, and reverted to its true function; while as the body grew more obedient, the spirit in proportion grew more free, as having an adequate instrument for all its uses at command. The realization of this ideal could not of course be accomplished without a struggle, and in that struggle the mortification of the body was carried

at times too far. But neither the theoretical nor
the practical excesses of particular ascetics can
conceal from us the general aim of the Christian
society at large ; which was to restore body and
soul to their true relation of harmonious unity, by
investing the body with the sacrosanctity of the
soul which it subserved. Hence we find in early
Christian teaching great stress laid on bodily
behaviour—sobriety, modesty, seemliness of pos-
ture and gesture and voice and dress,—gentle
manners, in short, of every kind, and upon every
occasion, as becoming the visible manifestation of
the Christian soul ; while the same thought, further
emphasized by the hope of resurrection, led to
increased tenderness and reverence in the treatment
of the dead. Thus the place of the body in human
personality, its intimate connexion with our inmost
self, and consequent participation in all the phases
of our moral and religious life, was recognized as it
had never been before.

Then there is the sacramental system to which
baptism and the eucharist gave rise. This was
not of course as elaborate at first as in process of
time it came to be ; nor do we find in the early
church those definitions and distinctions to which
subsequent controversy led. But we see clearly that
from the very first, the material elements of these
two sacraments were intimately connected in the
Christian consciousness with the grace which they

conveyed. The early fathers dwell not only on baptism, but on the water of baptism, that 'water united to the word,' as Clement calls it (ὕδωρ λογικόν), 'the blessed sacrament of water' (*felix sacramentum aquae*), which has an angel of its own like that of Bethesda, in Tertullian's belief. Tertullian indeed goes so far as to say of his own treatise upon baptism, 'I am afraid that I may seem rather to have been accumulating the praises of water than the reasons for baptism.' It is once called by Origen a symbol; but plainly for most it was more than this—a symbol penetrated and transfused by the illuminating presence of what it symbolized, and therefore a holy thing. So too with the eucharistic elements. Ignatius call the eucharist 'the flesh of our Saviour Jesus Christ.' Justin Martyr, 'no common bread or drink . . . but the flesh and blood of the incarnate Jesus.' Irenaeus, 'no longer common bread, but the eucharist, consisting of two things, an earthly and a heavenly.' 'We are distressed,' says Tertullian, 'if aught of the chalice or bread fall upon the ground.' Such expressions would have to be qualified, if we were discussing the precise doctrine of the early church, by others from Clement, Origen, and the Greek fathers; but they suffice to show from how early a date the material elements of the eucharist were regarded as, to say the least, of a peculiar sanctity, though its precise nature had not as yet been

critically defined. Here then we have a parallel to
the Christian view of the human body—water and
bread and wine, raised to a position of new dignity
as vehicles of a spiritual benediction upon men;
while the entire dependence of their value, upon
the spirit with which they were linked, is at the
same time clearly and emphatically maintained.

But these new sacraments had, as we have seen,
like all things else, a history. They date back to
primaeval religion, and are the offspring of earlier
rites; rites which in the course of ages had acquired
their appropriate ceremonial. Hence it was not
unnatural that in the process of time the Christian
sacraments should attract to themselves the acces-
sories of Jewish and Graeco-Roman worship; postures, gestures, vestments, sacred symbols and
utensils, solemn processions, religious music, incense,
chrism, lights; raising the old-world ritual to a higher
and holier use. It is of course easy from a modern
point of view to regard this process as retrogressive;
a return from Christian spirituality to Jewish and
pagan materialism. But as a matter of fact, this is
far too narrow and unsympathetic a judgement.
All religion as it becomes popular is apt to be
degraded; and the Christian sacraments were undoubtedly degraded in their popular use. But on
the other hand, all religion has and must have its
material side. This material side of religion is its
body, its necessary organ of expression and mani-

festation, and has persisted in unbroken continuity from the earliest days. Every successive religion has entered upon some part or other of this common heritage, this great ritual tradition; elevating, inspiring, improving, it may be, but still using the time-honoured forms. And Christianity, with its world-wide appeal to all races and classes of mankind, could be no exception to the rule. Moreover the Incarnation was, by its very nature, as we have been arguing above, the final sanction and justification of this great principle in things; the extreme recognition of the fact that the all spiritual truth must be embodied in material form. Had Christianity been merely a spiritual religion—supposing such a thing possible—and subsequently adopted sacraments, this might conceivably have been called a decline. But the religion of the Incarnation could not possibly be merely spiritual. It not only started with sacraments from its very origin; but it was essentially and fundamentally sacramental to the core. For what is the Incarnation itself but a sacrament, the sum and substance of all sacraments? When therefore theologians called baptism and the eucharist extensions of the Incarnation, they were using no rhetorical metaphors; they were literally and accurately correct. For these ordinances, with the sacramental network which insensibly gathered round them, were the means and witness of that consecration of the body, as an integral element in our whole personality, which it had been the work of the Incarnation to effect. And it was inevitable, in accordance with all laws of historic evolution, that these sacraments once instituted, should gradually clothe themselves with the colours and associations of those earlier rites which, in the deepest sense, they came not to destroy but to fulfil. Thus the growth of the sacramental system was an historical necessity; which, despite of the religious materialism into which it too frequently lapsed, was part and parcel of that great reclamation of the material world for God, which began with the Word made Flesh.

And this naturally leads our thoughts to the influence of Christianity upon art. The connexion of art and religion was a thing of immemorial age :—

'Pictores quis nescit ab Iside pasci.'

And we are not surprised to see how soon, in the catacombs, art was pressed into the Christian service. But fierce controversies had to rage, before art was made finally at home in the Church. The Iconoclasts felt its danger, and protested against its use, with a puritan austerity which cannot but command our respect. But Iconoclasm was foredoomed to failure by the very nature of the case. For what has been said of the sacramental system applies equally to art. The Incarnation involved artistic development as part of its redemption of the material world, its restoration of matter to the service of the spirit. And accordingly the note of all great Christian art is the subordination of material beauty to spiritual use. Of course all Christian art was not great; and where religion was degenerate or taste degraded, we meet with bloodstained crucifixions and realistic martyrdoms which are as hideously inartistic as they are alien to the true spirit of Christianity. And equally, of course, all great art was not Christian; when pursued, in modern phrase, for art's sake, colour and form and impression becoming ends in themselves. But this does not alter the fact that the religion of the Incarnation breathed a new life into art, and endowed it with new power over the thoughts and affections of men.

First and foremost there are the Gothic cathedrals,

'Everlasting piles
Types of the spiritual church which God hath
   reared.

.   .   .   .   .   .

Where bubbles burst, and folly's dancing foam
Melts, if it cross the threshold; where the wreath
Of awe-struck wisdom droops[1].'

Stone seems in them to lose its stubborn nature, as it soars, in obedience, tier over tier, to the infinite aspiration of the soul.

'With living wiles
Instinct—to rouse the heart and lead the will
By a bright ladder to the world above[1].'

[1] Wordsworth, *Ecclesiastical Sketches*.

They are perhaps the most striking instance of spirit's power to subdue matter, since it is matter of the most obstinate, concrete, solid kind which is thus subdued.   But the same is the case with Christian painting, in a still subtler degree; Cimabue, Giotto, and their followers not only raised and dignified pictorial art, by their dedication of brush and pencil to the Christian service; but, in so doing, they discovered in it new depths of possibility, wholly unsuspected capacities of spiritual expression, fresh powers in the sensuous image to show the innermost secrets of the soul.

> ' The early painters,
> To cries of " Greek Art and what more wish
>   you ? "
> Replied, " To become now self-acquainters,
>   And paint man, man, whatever the issue!
> Make new hopes shine through the flesh they fray,
>   New fears aggrandize the rags and tatters:
> To bring the invisible full into play!
>   Let the visible go to the dogs—what matters ?[1] " '

It is the same, again, with music, which may be called pre-eminently the Christian art.   For whatever earlier traditions paved the way for it, the development of music from the Gregorian age to that of Handel and Bach, was virtually a new creation.   It arose out of the Christian worship, under

---

[1] Browning, *Old Pictures in Florence.*

the Christian inspiration, and was matured by Christian artists, and for Christian use. Not unnaturally therefore it is the art in which matter is most completely subordinate to spirit. For sound, as it floats upon the viewless air, can scarcely be called a material thing. Its mechanical origin is forgotten in its invisible effect. And when these airy, unsubstantial, wandering tones are caught by the musician and transfigured with the magic of his art, they seem to lose the last lingering remnant of material restraint. Wherever the spirit ranges, music is free to follow. No joy is too ecstatic, no sorrow too deep, no action too impetuous, no passion too intense, no phase of thought or feeling too rare, to come within its scope. It thrills and throbs with every movement of the life which it interprets and reveals. And we feel that matter can go no further ; it has reached its limit ; it has become, as Hegel truly says, independent of space and time :—

'*Miscrere, Domine!*
The words are utter'd, and they flee.
Deep is their penitential moan,
Mighty their pathos, but 'tis gone.
They have declared the spirit's sore
Sore load, and words can do no more.
Beethoven takes them then—those two
Poor, bounded words—and makes them new ;
Infinite makes them, makes them young ;
Transplants them to another tongue,

Where they can now, without constraint,
Pour all the soul of their complaint,
And roll adown a channel large
The wealth divine they have in charge.
Page after page of music turn,
And still they live and still they burn,
Perennial, passion-fraught, and free—
Miserere, Domine ! [1]'

The arts indeed as they have reached their maturity, have acquired an independent life of their own; and are no longer so obviously connected with the Christian worship, or illumined by the Christian faith, as once they were. But this apparent secularity, if art can ever be called secular, must not blind us to the essential sacredness of all true art, and to the fact that it arose in sacred places, and was destined for a sacred use. It is, as we now possess it, a gift of Christianity to the world ; just as our common morality which is now public property, the possession of believers and unbelievers alike,—and which is often credited, in consequence, with a secular origin—really grew up under Christian influence, and was fostered by Christian devotion till it grew strong enough in the end to stand alone.

Thus the religion of the Incarnation raised the sacramental and artistic capabilities of matter to

---

[1] Matthew Arnold, *Epilogue to Lessing's Laocoon.*

a new level, as it raised the human body itself; making them minister to that 'coming of the kingdom of God,' that development of a society of holy persons, whose object was to regenerate the world.

Hence the religious effect of art and sacrament is the reproduction, on a higher plane, of that same influence which we have seen the mere spectacle of the world to exert. It is the religious influence of material nature, focussed, localized, intensified, by the conscious intervention of man ; precisely as the natural forces of heat and light and electricity are focussed and localized by human agency, to be turned to human use.

It follows that the spiritual influence of art and sacrament must be as real—in modern phrase as objectively real—as that of nature, which they do but emphasize. We have argued at length that the religious influence of nature is too obviously real to be attributed to mere subjective sentiment, mere feeling without objective counterpart; and that it must be conceived of as the divine omnipresence making itself felt. When therefore we emphasize this presence, either by the help of inspired genius as in the arts, or in a higher and more solemn way, by celebration of the sacraments ordained by Christ, the like reality must attach to those points of emphasis. Carlyle speaks of art as 'eternity looking through time'; Newman of music as 'the outpourings of eternal harmony in the medium of created sound'; Browning as

> 'A flash of the will that can,
> Existent behind all laws, that made them, and
>   lo they are [1].'

And these are more than rhetorical phrases. They express the common conviction of serious minds, that just as science does not invent but discovers the laws of the material world, so art does not create but reveals the truth of spiritual things. There is a spiritual power in the universe to illuminate our minds, to enkindle our hearts, and to stir our wills; and the genius of the artist is among the instruments through which this spirit speaks.

And what is true of art is from the Christian point of view still more true of sacraments. We cannot indeed, and need not, define the method of their operation, as rival theologians have so often attempted to do. For we know nothing of the ulti-mate nature of either of their elements, nor how those elements, even in our own persons, are com-bined. And this is the point which is really involved, rather than any strictly theological issue, in all the various sacramental theories, which lie between the poles of Zwingli and the Council of Trent. But, however we regard them, the fact remains that the sacraments were selected and

[1] Browning, *Abt Vogler.*

ordained by Christ to be means, in one way or another, of union and communion with Himself. Had they been arbitrarily chosen things, we might perhaps have been content to call them symbols. But they are very far indeed, as we have seen, from being arbitrary inventions. They have a history behind them as old as humanity, and a context around them as wide as the world ; and point us back to sacramental customs of immemorial age. And if these earlier rites derived reality and value from God's immanence in the world, and found Him at particular times and places because He is everywhere present and ready to be found, the Christian sacraments must possess this reality in its highest degree. While in their case it is further fortified by the fact that they are divine commands ; and carry with them the direct promise of a personal response to the personal allegiance which they claim ; the promise not that God may be found, but that He will definitely meet us, at the time and in the place of His appointment. Thus the sacraments, in our Christian view of them, are the key to the material world, as the means of union with the supreme reality, the personal God ; while the form of them—an ablution and a meal —our simplest bodily needs—reminds us that our bodies are an integral element in that entire personality, whose destiny is union with the Word made Flesh.

CHAPTER VII

THE INCARNATION AND THE TRINITY

IT will have been observed that the preceding pages are in no way intended to summarize the general evidence for the truth of the Incarnation; which is a thing that must be studied in its full detail in order to be felt with its full weight. Their object in dealing with the Incarnation has merely been to vindicate and emphasize one of its aspects; its place, namely, in our philosophy of nature, its relation to our conviction of God's immanence in the natural world. But all attempts to present religious doctrine in a philosophical connexion run a certain risk of conveying the impression that it is only philosophical—a speculative suggestion, an intellectual after-thought, an unsubstantial vision in the air. And such impression is doubly dangerous, in the present day, from the fact, that it may seem to give colour to the commonest form of contemporaneous attack on Christianity; which represents the Incarnation, with the Trinitarian theology that it involves, as metaphysical corruptions of what was once a simpler creed. It may be advisable therefore, as a safeguard, as well as a confirmation of what has gone before, to point out the practical character of both these doctrines, as well as the practical method of their introduction to the world.

'Faithful souls,' says St. Hilary of Poitiers, 'would be contented with the word of God, which bids us " Go teach all nations, baptizing them in the name of the Father, and of the Son, and of the Holy Ghost." ' 'But alas!' he continues, 'we are driven by the faults of our heretical opponents to do things unlawful, to scale heights inaccessible, to speak out what is unspeakable, to presume where we ought not. And whereas it is by faith alone that we should worship the Father, and reverence the Son, and be filled with the Spirit, we are now obliged to strain our weak human language in the utterance of things beyond its scope ; forced into this evil procedure by the evil procedure of our foes. Hence, what should be matter of silent religious meditation must now needs be imperilled by exposition in words.'

This passage is from the first great dogmatic treatise of the Christian Church, that of St. Hilary on the Trinity ; and it is admirably typical of the patristic attitude towards all dogmatic definition. The fathers, unlike the schoolmen, had no love of it ; they recognized its occasional necessity, but recognized it, for the most part, with regret ; and never without a sense that the ground they trod was holy ground, the mysteries they handled, things of awe. Accordingly, it will be noticed that Hilary here, like Augustine after him, bases the doctrine of the Trinity entirely on a simple fact,— namely, the baptismal formula of the Christian Church ; which from the first must have carried with it some traditional interpretation, yet which confessedly has nothing metaphysical about it. This form of words presided over the greatest change that has occurred in history, and it is obvious that sooner or later it would have had to be explained. But the process of this explanation lies open before us in its every stage ; and it is perfectly plain that from first to last it was regarded as the interpretation of a revealed fact. The incessant appeal is to what the Scripture says, or what the saying of the Scripture means. No speculative element is introduced at any point : and the resulting creeds are nothing more than the authorized epitomes of what, in the view of their composers, the Gospels contain. Concrete facts, when they are translated into the terms of science or philosophy, look very unlike themselves. A daisy, for example, is not like its botanical description, nor a sonata like its musical score. And so the simple password that gives entrance to a world-wide family, will naturally differ from the intellectual statement of what a great religion means.

Viewed, then, in the light of its history, the doctrine of the Trinity is no metaphysical invention like the Platonic 'ideas,' or the Aristotelian 'form'; but simply the expression in philosophical language of what had entered the world as a statement of fact—the fact that there is plurality, triune plurality in God. And though at first sight this might seem a mystery too transcendental to be worth revelation, its revelation was in fact a thing of the profoundest practical import.

'I am come that they might have life,' said Jesus Christ, 'and that they might have it more abundantly.' Truer, fuller, fairer life is the ultimate issue of the religion of the cross; no mere theory, but a plain, palpable, practical result. Yet the entire possibility of this result depended upon such an increased knowledge of God's nature as should enable a clearer comprehension of His whole relationship to man. 'God is loving,' had been said by others before the time of Jesus Christ, but never 'God is Love': and there is a world of difference between the two propositions. The statement of the psalmist, that 'God is loving unto every man,' does not of necessity imply that love is more than what may be called a relative and secondary attribute of God; an affection elicited by the existence, the ephemeral existence of His creatures, and which, apart from that existence, would cease to operate, and therefore to be. God in His unknown essence might still be something other than Love: but the statement that 'God is Love' is very different from this: it is a real revelation beyond all that we could otherwise have learned: it lifts Love at once into the absolute, as the essential and eternal cause of all; thereby exhibiting the whole world in a new light. For there is all the difference between a mysterious, unintelligible universe, whose fathomless depths are never pierced by the uncertain gleams of love, which play fitfully from time to time upon their face; and one whose first and final cause, whose very root and ground is love; one amid whose mysteries we can therefore move with confidence, and whose unsolved problems we can face with hope.

But if love is to be thought of as thus absolute, or in other words synonymous with God, as distinct from being merely contingent on creation, there must of necessity be conceived a plurality of persons in the Godhead; for when we speak of love we mean the affection of one person for another, and except it be taken in that sense, the word is utterly and blankly meaningless. If, therefore, the proclamation that God is Love does not mean this, it has no more value or significance than that the unknown is the unknowable.

Hence if human life was to be renewed, and human society reconstructed on the basis of the faith that 'God is Love,' there was paramount need that enough of the veil should be lifted from the Godhead, to assure us that those words really meant what they must inevitably appear to mean. Thus, what is often misrepresented as a speculative superfluity turns out upon analysis to be the most practical of truths.

To say this is not, of course, to imply that intellectual illumination was the primary object of the Christian religion, but merely that Christianity could not have been taught along the ages, without some such illumination of the intellect as that by which, in fact, it was accompanied.

Hence this illumination has always been regarded as an integral portion of the Christian Creed, enhancing and not diminishing its practical efficiency, by including head as well as heart in its appeal. For it supplies us with an analogy that we can follow out in thought. The fairest thing we know on earth, the truest practical solution of life's problem, is a society or family whose members are united by a common bond of love. Within the charmed circle, such love is reflected from each to all and all to each, and gathers in the process an intimate intensity, far beyond all power to express; while, to those who are without, it ever burns to impart some fragment of its own inspiring energy and joy,

by thoughts of tenderness and words of sympathy,
and deeds of kindly care.

Here, then, we have a picture drawn from the
noblest thing we know, which illustrates, however
feebly, the Christian doctrine of the Trinity, that
Divine Society, whose co-equal members are one in
infinite eternal love, and who in that love's exuber-
ance come forth, in a sense, from out themselves, to
create, to sustain, to redeem, to sanctify, to bless.

It must not for a moment be supposed that we
can follow this analogy in detail, or that it does
not still leave much that is obscure. The human
picture melts away into the light that no man
can approach unto. The Father remains incomprehensible, the Son incomprehensible, and the Holy
Ghost incomprehensible. Such has always been
the language of the Church. In a word, her doctrine
is sufficient to make our thought of God more full,
more real, more adequate to influence human life;
while in contrast with all philosophies which attempt to criticize the Absolute, it leaves His
ineffable mystery alone. Those philosophies, on
the other hand, have never succeeded in presenting
us with either a likelier or a clearer conception of
God ; while in power to control conduct, to console
sorrow, to develop life, they are immeasurably sur-
passed by the Christian creed.

And this is after all the true test of a theology ;
the extent and character of its influence on life.

For no modern form of Theism views God as
a mere logical abstraction, whose unity can only
be maintained by isolation from the world. However variously men think about Him, in the present
day, they would at least agree, that He must be
regarded as the real, concrete, source and ground
and goal of things ; by His intimate, immanent
omnipresence making the universe one whole, or in
older language, ' upholding all things ' and ' filling
all in all.'

But foremost in the universe of our experience is
man. God, even if we call Him the unknown, must
yet be the source and ground and goal of human
personality, and all its powers. If therefore He is
to control His universe, He must be able to control
man in the precise way in which man's nature
instinctively demands to be controlled, that is, by
personal influence. Hence He must Himself at
least be personal. ' Supra-personal ' is thought by
some to be more descriptive of a personality that
must infinitely transcend our own. And the term
may be permissible, if it is clearly understood to
imply the inclusion of the essential attributes of
personality ; as we might call chemical phenomena supra-mechanical, or vital phenomena supra-
chemical ; meaning that in each case the higher
order included and utilized the lower. But in
fact the term ' supra-personal ' is often taken to
imply such an absorption of personality as would

obliterate its distinctive features; much as water in absorbing a crystal destroys its unity and form. In this sense the word is merely a disguised, and therefore misleading synonym, for the plainer term 'impersonal,' of which it must in consequence share the fate.

To resume then, any adequate notion that we can form of God must include the capacity for influencing persons; and persons, in the last resort, can only be influenced by love. For appeals to the reason, and even appeals to the conscience, are partial in their effect, and do not comprehend the entire man. But appeals to the heart compel the allegiance of our whole personality; and are more-over the sole form of compulsion to which a being endowed with freedom, can, without loss of his integrity, submit. If therefore God is to be master of the human element in His universe, He must be so by appealing to its love.

> ' For the loving worm within its clod,
>   Were diviner than a loveless god
>   Amid his worlds, I will dare to say[1].'

Hence the superiority of the Christian to all other theologies. The God of Plato, the God of Aristotle, the God of Spinoza, cannot appeal to the heart. They cannot hold the universe together, for there is a thing in the universe which eludes their

[1] Browning, *Christmas Eve*.

grasp; and to that extent, therefore, at least, they are not gods. The same may be said of all unitarian or Sabellian conceptions. They leave no room for attributing love, in any intelligible sense, to the divine nature; and cannot therefore satisfy the craving of humanity for union with a Being who loves because He must, who loves because His essence is love. Love, in a word, is the sole solution of life's problem; and the doctrine of the Trinity is the sole metaphysic of love. Of course if it were only a metaphysical theory, it would have no advantage, except that of greater probability, over other theories; but its distinction is that it did not enter the world in theoretic but in practical form.

Jesus Christ came speaking in simplest language of the love of God; and then of Himself, to an inner circle, as the proof and exhibition of that love; and then of those relationships within the Godhead which made His Incarnation possible in fact, and capable of being in a measure comprehended in thought. And there is congruity in this. True love does not speak without acting; and the proclamation that God is love would have been self-contradictory, if it had not been accompanied by its own practical proof. The fact of the Incarnation came first, and then its doctrine; but the two involve and presuppose each other. Now men forget this fact when they speak lightly of the doctrine of the Trinity, as if it were a mere speculative paradox, wholly out of relation to the practical needs of a practical age ; they forget that it supports and is supported by the whole weight of a fact in history, with which nothing else in the wide world can even for a moment be compared. That fact is the age-long empire of Jesus Christ over the hearts of men. The picture of that empire has been drawn with unrivalled power, and its significance pressed home with unanswerable logic by the great French preacher of our age; but nevertheless in much current controversy its evidential value is ignored. Yet there it is, an unique fact, that has lasted now through nineteen centuries, and is, without question, as energetic in the world to-day, as in any bygone age. The survey of man's nature assures us that its only key is love, and we are forced to infer that if God controls the universe by laws appropriate to its modes of being, He must draw humanity by the cords of a man, that is by the law of love. One has come, claiming to be God made manifest,—manifest in order to attract our love. He has attracted and retained it :—'with limitations,' it will be said. Yes, with limitations, but limitations which Himself predicted as exactly as He predicted the attraction that should know no end. So that, in fact, the perpetual miracle of the love that He inspires is enhanced by the prophetic power that foretold its course.

M

This then is the position of the Christian theology. It presents us with a doctrine of God, which, while claiming to be revealed, justifies the claim by being clearer than any adverse view. And moreover it presents this doctrine supported by a great historic fact—the greatest, the most wonderful, the most important fact in history. This fact, the empire of Christ, so supernatural and yet so human, presupposes the truth of the doctrine, and could not otherwise have come to pass ; while on the other hand the doctrine finds its natural, its necessary outcome in the historical occurrence of the fact.

Now this is a combination of theory and practice, thought and thing, that should appeal with especial power to the mind of a practical age. For practical men, who are in any sense to be worthy of the name, will be the first to admit that action presupposes reflection, practice rests on principle ; while success in our active efforts is the gauge and guarantee of soundness in the thoughts from which they spring. Hence the supremacy of the Christian religion in the field of practical achievement should commend, to men of action, the central doctrine it involves.

That it has been, and is, so supreme in achievement, few serious thinkers will deny. For it has inspired a love which, both in kind and degree, remains, as we have seen, unique. It has quickened by its presence all the forces that make for progress, even in what are called the secular movements of the world: while among the dim sad things of life, which no secular progress can remove—poverty, pain, shame, sorrow, doubt, despondency, and death, —it reigns, as the great consoler, incontestably alone.

What then is the real root of the objection to the doctrine of the Trinity and the Incarnation, if it is neither speculative improbability, nor want of practical support? There can be little doubt that the secret cause of its unpopularity consists in its claim to be a revelation from God. Such a claim of course cannot fail to provoke antagonism in many minds, by the demand upon character and conduct which it inevitably makes; and this antagonism may exist as an unconscious bias even among men, who, without being otherwise immoral, yet shrink from the spiritual progress that a definite revelation is felt to imply. But apart from this moral drawback, common to all ages, modern thinkers have an objection of their own. The unity of nature, they urge, and the uniform action of its laws, create a presumption against personal divine interference, of which unscientific minds and ages cannot appreciate the weight. Without further pausing on the philosophical criticism to which this argument is open, it will be sufficient for our present purpose to call attention to one fact. Nature includes human nature; and

"Man, once descried, imprints for ever
His presence on all lifeless things."

Human nature is an integral portion of our sum total of experience; and while comprising instances within itself of all the classes of phenomena, that nature elsewhere exhibits in a wider way— mechanism, chemistry, energy, organization, life— it possesses other characteristics which are peculiarly its own. And while the study of external nature is confessedly a thing of yesterday, the study of the human spirit is as old as its records of itself, and has been conducted by many a genius, before which modern names grow pale.

Now religious instincts and aspirations are, as is perfectly well known, among the deepest, the most universal, the most essential attributes of man. These instincts, from time immemorial, have craved a revelation, and the Christian revelation meets and satisfies this craving, in a manner and a measure that are alike unique. At least then it is entitled to the same consideration as would be accorded to a scientific theory, in parallel case. Modern science is familiar with theories, which are far from possibility of proof, and yet, from their correspondence with the facts of experience, are regarded as practically true. We may reasonably claim therefore that if tested, as we test other hypotheses, the Christian revelation stands in similar case. It fits the facts within its province, as no other scheme

can fit them; and that, without conflicting with
any other kinds of fact: whereas its rivals are all
partial, and however much they may explain, leave
life, and love, and death, and spiritual experience
unexplained.   Yet if the world can be explained at
all, and is therefore rational, as all science is bound
to maintain, its highest product, the human spirit,
must be rational and explicable too; and some
answer to its aspirations, some solution of its
problems must exist.   Why should not the one
answer which has appeared, and is adequate, be
true?

'So, the All-Great, were the All-Loving too—
So, through the thunder comes a human voice
Saying, "O heart I made, a heart beats here!
Face, my hands fashioned, see it in myself,
Thou hast no power nor may'st conceive of mine,
But love I gave thee, with myself to love,
And thou must love me who have died for thee![1]"'

---

[1] Browning, *An Epistle.*

APPENDIX

I. PERSONAL IDENTITY

'A PERSON,' says Reid, 'is something indivisible, and is what Leibnitz calls a *monad*. My personal identity, therefore, implies the continued existence of that indivisible thing which I call myself. Whatever this self may be, it is something which thinks, and deliberates, and resolves, and acts, and suffers. I am not thought, I am not action, I am not feeling; I am something that thinks, and acts, and suffers. My thoughts, and actions, and feelings, change every moment—they have no continued, but a successive existence; but that self or I, to which they belong, is permanent, and has the same relation to all the succeeding thoughts, actions, and feelings, which I call mine. . . . The proper evidence I have of all this is remembrance.

'The conviction which every man has of his identity, as far back as his memory reaches, needs no aid of philosophy to strengthen it; and no philosophy can weaken it, without first producing

some degree of insanity.   We probably at first
derive our notion of identity from that natural
conviction which every man has from the dawn of
reason of his own identity and continued existence.
The identity which we ascribe to bodies . . . is not
perfect identity. . . . It admits of a great change
of subject, provided the change be gradual. . . .
But identity, when applied to persons, has no ambi-
guity, and admits not of degrees, or of more and
less.   It is the foundation of all rights and obliga-
tions, and of all accountableness, and the notion of
it is fixed and precise.'   (REID, *Intell. Powers*, iii.
c. 4.)

'When it is asked,' says Butler, 'wherein personal
identity consists, the answer should be the same, as
if it were asked, wherein consists similitude, or
equality; that all attempts to define would but
perplex it.   Yet there is no difficulty at all in
ascertaining the idea.   For as, upon two triangles
being compared or viewed together, there arises to
the mind the idea of similitude ; or upon twice two
and four, the idea of equality: so likewise, upon
comparing the consciousnesses of one's self, or one's
own existence, in any two moments, there as immediately arises to the mind the idea of personal
identity. . . . And though the successive consciousnesses, which we have of our own existence, are not
the same, yet are they consciousnesses of one and

the same thing or object; of the same person, self, or living agent. The person, of whose existence the consciousness is felt now, and was felt an hour or a year ago, is discerned to be, not two persons, but one and the same person ; and therefore is one and the same. . . . And one should really think it self-evident, that consciousness of personal identity presupposes, and therefore cannot constitute, personal identity ; any more than knowledge, in any other case, can constitute truth, which it presupposes.' (*Of Personal Identity.*)

The above passages indicate with sufficient clearness what we mean by personal identity. It is a fact, thus understood, of every sane man's inner experience, an ultimate fact which we cannot get behind. Common sense and sound metaphysic are agreed upon the point. But there is a vague notion, in some quarters, that the conception of personal identity as thus described, has been discredited by the investigations of physiological psychology. It may be well therefore to point out why this is not, and, in the nature of things, cannot be the case. And this will perhaps best be seen if we confront with the above passages a typical statement of the physiological point of view, from M. Ribot's *Diseases of Personality.*

'The organism and the brain, as its highest representation, constitute the real personality, containing in itself all that we have been and the possibilities of all that we shall be. The whole individual character is inscribed there with all its active and passive aptitudes, sympathies, and antipathies; its genius, talents, or stupidity; its virtues, vices, torpor, or activity. What emerges and reaches consciousness is little only compared with what lies buried below, albeit still active. Conscious personality is never more than a feeble portion of physical personality. The unity of the ego, accordingly, is not that of the single entity of spiritualists, dispersing itself into multiple phenomena, but the co-ordination of a certain number of incessantly renascent states, having for their sole support the vague sense of the body. This unity does not pass from above to below, but from below to above; it is not an initial, but a terminal point. . . . The unity of the ego, in a psychological sense, is, accordingly, the cohesion, during a given period, of a certain number of distinct states of consciousness, accompanied by others less distinct, and by a multitude of physiological states which, though not accompanied by consciousness like the others, yet operate as powerfully as they, if not more so. Unity means co-ordination.' (RIBOT, *Diseases of Personality*, Eng. Trans.)

Now the experience which this passage attempts to explain away, is, as above stated, a fact of our

internal consciousness : but the evidence on which
the explanation rests, is a collection of external observations—observations of different organic functions, effects of physical temperament, bodily moods,
perversions of sensibility, monstrous births, diseases,
insanity, hypnotic conditions, and the like.

It will be obvious at a glance, therefore, that
the entire passage is, from first to last, *a petitio
principii*. It begs the question at issue; as has
always been the case, since the days when Cud-
worth said of Hobbes and his followers, they ' do
plainly dance round in a circle.' For the gulf
between our knowledge of matter and our knowledge of spirit is impassable. From the outside
we can never see a movement think; and from
the inside we can never feel a thought move. And
as long as this is the case, we can tell absolutely
nothing of the ultimate nature of their relationship.
But this gulf, in the passage before us, is leaped at
a bound, ' The organism constitutes the personality.'
. . . ' The unity is not that of the spiritualists.' . . .
' The unity of the ego is the cohesion,' &c. Each
of these phrases is an assertion that there is no
more in the spiritual element of personality than
can be discerned from the material side. And
this is no accidental illogicality of the particular
writer; it is inherent in his point of view. Any
attempt to dissolve the unity, which we only know
as a fact of internal consciousness, into elements

which we only know as facts of external observation, must beg the question.

As a matter of fact, the more cautious psychologists are aware of this, as the following passages from Höffding may show :—

' Even though the individual organism, which in spite of its completeness and relative independence is still a republic of cells, were to be explained as compounded out of elements, and its origin made intelligible through the law of the persistence of energy, this would not explain the individual consciousness, the formation of a special centre of memory, of action, and of suffering. That it is possible for such an inner centre to come into being is the fundamental problem of all our knowledge. Each individual trait, each individual property, might perhaps be explained by the power of heredity and the influence of experience ; but the inner unity, to which all elements refer, and by virtue of which the individuality is a *psychical* individuality, remains for us an eternal riddle. . . . It is impossible to apply to the mental province anything analogous to the persistence of energy. Psychical individuality is one of the practical limits of science.'

' The peculiarity of the phenomena of consciousness, as contrasted with the subject-matter of the

science of external nature—material phenomena—
is precisely that inner connexion between the
individual elements in virtue of which they appear
as belonging to one and the same subject.'

'Physiology, like every natural science, explains
a material process by means of other material
processes. Its assumptions are not framed to include
a case in which one member of the causal relation
shall be spatial, the other non-spatial.'

'Mental existence . . . has for its fundamental
form, memory, synthesis; and synthesis presupposes
individuality. The material world shows us no
real individualities, these are first known to the
psychological standpoint, from which inner centres
of memory, action, and endurance are discovered.'

'In recognition and in memory is expressed an
inner unity, to which the material world affords no
parallel.' (HÖFFDING, *Outlines of Psychology, Eng.
Trans.*)

These statements are especially noteworthy, as
coming from an empirical psychologist.

But it may be urged that though not logically
demonstrable, the physical analysis of personality
rests on so many analogies as to be highly probable.
This again cannot be maintained as long as the
gulf in question remains unbridged. For the two
sets of facts have nothing in common, and no

analogy can extend from one region to the other. Compare Professor T. H. Green :—

'If the function relative to our consciousness, which belongs to neural process, were involved in our consciousness in the same way in which chemical processes are involved in those of animal life, every step gained in our acquaintance with this function would also advance our knowledge of consciousness. But it is not so. There is no continuance of neural process into our consciousness as there is of chemical processes into life. Life is indeed more and other than chemical changes; these changes only contribute to it in a living organism; but they do enter into it, are ascertainable elements in it. If chemistry cannot tell us how the living body is constructed, it yet can tell us of what it is constructed. If we analyze the growth of a tissue, or the formation of the blood, into its constituent processes, we find at any rate among these such as are strictly chemical. It may not be a complete account of the origin of animal heat to say that it results from the union of oxygen, derived through respiration from the atmosphere, with the carbon contained in certain food-stuffs; but there is no doubt that such oxidation is a constituent in its production. But when we analyze any determination or mode of consciousness, we do not come upon neural tremors. If we take the physiologist's consciousness of the function of the brain, or the musician's of a tune which he "carries in his head," and inquire what are its constituents, what are the conditions which together make it what it is, it is with ideas or determinations of consciousness that we are left in the last resort. Nothing that the physiologist can detect —no irritation, no irradiation, or affection of a sensitive organ—enters into it at all. The relations which these terms represent are all of a kind absolutely heterogeneous to, and incompatible with, the mutual determination of ideas in the unity of consciousness. They all imply distinctions of space and time which that unity perhaps renders possible, but which it excludes from itself.' (GREEN, *Phil. Works,* i. 475.)

And again,—

'The sentient organism is not in any proper sense the subject of the feelings to which it is organic. It is not conscious of them as its feelings. If the expression may be pardoned, it is not an *it* for itself at all, but only for us. The apparatus of nerve and tissue has no unity for itself, but only for us, to whom it presents itself as one in virtue of its function. Its unity means merely the combined action of many elements, in relation to one irresoluble effect, viz. feeling. The conversion of successive feelings into an experience, on the other hand, implies a subject

consciously relating them to itself, and at once
rendering them a manifold (which in themselves, as
successively vanishing, they are not), and unifying
this manifold by means of that relation. Such a subject has or is the unity which, under the name of
our understanding, enables us to find community
of function in the elements of the sentient organism,
and which thus renders it, derivatively, one for us.
To imagine an "evolution" of the self-conscious
subject from the gathered experience of the sentient
organism—an evolution of the unifying agent from
that which it renders one—is the last form which the
standing ὕστερον πρότερον of empirical psychology
has assumed.' (GREEN, *Works*, i. 466.)

The first objection therefore to our regarding
personality as a mere product of the bodily organism is, that the attempt to do so involves a logical
fallacy. But there is a more important metaphysical
objection to which Professor Green alludes, in the
above passages, and which it is the especial object
of his elaborate criticism of the empirical psychology
to exhibit. Briefly it is, that all knowledge of
objects must presuppose a subject; which cannot
therefore be derived from the things of whose intelligibility it is itself the constitutive condition. This
is very clearly put by Lotze, in a passage which
I have quoted elsewhere; but whose importance may
justify its repetition in the present context.

'It has been required of any theory which starts
without presuppositions and from the basis of experience, that in the beginning it should speak only
of sensations or ideas, without mentioning the soul
to which, it is said, we hasten without justification to
ascribe them.   I should maintain, on the contrary,
that such a mode of setting out involves a wilful
departure from that which is actually given in experience.   A mere sensation without a subject is
nowhere to be met with as a fact.   It is impossible
to speak of a bare movement without thinking of
the mass whose movement it is ; and it is just as
impossible to conceive a sensation existing without
the accompanying idea of that which has it—or,
rather, of that which feels it ; for this also is included in the given fact of experience that the
relation of the feeling subject to its feeling, whatever its other characteristics may be, is in any case
something different from the relation of the moved
element to its movement.   It is thus, and thus only,
that the sensation is a given fact ; and we have no
right to abstract from its relation to its subject
because this relation is puzzling, and because we
wish to obtain a starting-point which looks more
convenient but is utterly unwarranted by experience.
. . . Any comparison of two ideas, which ends by
our finding their contents like or unlike, presupposes
the absolutely indivisible unity of that which com-
pares them. . . . And so our whole inner world of

N

thoughts is built up; not as a mere collection of manifold ideas existing with or after one another, but as a world in which these individual members are held together and arranged by the relating activity of this single pervading principle.   This then is what we mean by the unity of consciousness; and it is this that we regard as the sufficient ground for assuming an indivisible soul.'   (*Metaphysic*, § 241.)

The result of Professor Green's analysis of Locke, Hume, Spencer, and Lewis (*Philosophical Works*, vol. i) is to show that this principle cannot be explained away without first being tacitly assumed; or in other words that it is the inevitable *prius* of all knowledge.   In brief he says :—

'The one consciousness, equally present to, yet distinguishing itself from, successive feelings, without which there could be no such synthesis of them as is necessary to a recognition of their difference in kind and degree, and to their constituting a consciousness of change, is first taken for granted and then represented as resulting from the synthesis which presupposes it.   It must be presupposed, in order to the possibility of feelings being held together as related by the subject which experiences them, and except as so held together they give no "materials for its establishment."'

One more statement of the case may be quoted, for its clearness, from Mr. D'Arcy :—

' Self-consciousness consists not merely in having feelings or thoughts, but in that consciousness which becomes explicit in the recognition of a feeling as " my " feeling, a thought as " my " thought, a book as the book which " I " see or touch or read. Self-consciousness is the strange power which the mind possesses of objectifying itself. It is implicit in all experience ; for, otherwise, experience is impossible. The unifying agency of the self, by which it passes from self to not-self and from every element in the not-self to every other element and combines all in one, is essentially the agency of self-consciousness. The subject is a unifying principle only in so far as it is self-conscious, i.e. in so far as it is able to rise above itself and its own opposition to the object. The objectified self is therefore no " group of mental states which form a permanent nucleus in the mental history." (ALEXANDER, *Moral Order and Progress*, p. 75.) No group of mental states could ever form a self in any but an improper (or derivative) sense of the term, for every group needs the self to constitute it, and in the very act of constituting it the self must be already implicitly self-conscious or the act could never take place. Self-consciousness is presupposed in the very formation of this so-called "empirical self." This empirical self is no more properly called " the self" than the body is properly called "the person."' (D'ARCY, *Short Study of Ethics*, p. 12.)

The difficulty that is often experienced in realizing the cogency of this reasoning arises simply from the fact of its being metaphysical. And some writers and thinkers have endeavoured accordingly to supplement it by empirical evidence, drawn from the phenomena of sleep, somnambulism, trance, and abnormal 'psychical' manifestations, and indicating the existence of a self or soul that is independent of the bodily organism. But this is an argument whose weight must, after all, be inevitably confined to those who have had sufficient experience of the evidence in question to be convinced by it. And though it may be useful as a counterblast to empiricism on the opposite side, it does not possess the rigorous necessity of metaphysical demonstration. For the point is essentially a metaphysical one—and its proper proof therefore is metaphysical. I can only use my faculties as I do, because I am a self-conscious being; and their use can neither create nor exhibit what is the necessary presupposition of their use; any more than my senses can create or exhibit, in the act and moment of my using them, the nervous mechanism on which they depend.

For a full treatment of the question, see Green (*Works*, vol. i), and for a further criticism of some recent writers, Ladd (*Philosophy of Mind*).

But it is in the moral region, as stated in the text, that our personal identity becomes most plain. Self-consciousness indeed is the necessary presupposition of self-determination, and therefore of morality, but it is in the concrete form of moral conduct that it is most easily recognized by the majority of men.   I am conscious of being morally responsible for what I remember doing ten, twenty, thirty, forty years ago.   I am certain that I am the same person who at those dates made a free choice between good and evil, and both this identity and this freedom place me in a category which—if the term nature is to be used as synonymous with the realm of physical causation—must be termed supernatural.   This again is a point which has been elaborately demonstrated by Professor Green in his *Prolegomena to Ethics*: and that it should be regarded by the empirical psychologists as an illusion (HÖFFDING, vii. B. 4) need not in any way disturb us, as this inevitably follows from their failure to recognize the true nature of the self-consciousness upon which it depends.

This permanent self then, which is the subject of all our thoughts, and which we know by self-consciousness, and can know in no other way, is the basis of our personality, in the sense of being that which makes us persons.   It is not our entire personality, when personality is used in the sense of concrete character, any more than the seed is the full-blown flower; but it is that which makes the development of our concrete character possible. And it would contribute to clearness of thought, if the term 'personality' were reserved to denote the quality of being a person, or self-conscious subject ; while 'mood' and 'character' are used to designate the particular state or kind of person. In popular language, for instance, we speak of a person in different moods of joy and sorrow as being quite a different person, but when Mr. Ribot does this in a scientific treatise, the result is destructive of all accurate thought.

A concrete person then, as he knows himself from within, is a self-conscious subject with a certain character, existing in connexion with a bodily organism. And though the bodily organism provides material for the formation of the character, it does not constitute it. A man is not the result of his bodily organism, but of the way in which he has reacted on his bodily organism ; in other words, of his will. The body has its appetites, its instincts, its hereditary tendencies, its idiosyncrasies of disposition and temperament, its nerves and cerebral impressions. But a man's character does not depend upon the mere existence of these things, but upon the use made of them ; the way in which some have been selected for encouragement, and others have been suppressed ; the particular portion of the total potentiality which has been voluntarily realized. And though it is quite true, of course, that there attach to every man a number of minor characteristics, which help to constitute his individuality, and yet have never been made objects of will, these are essentially subordinate to, and qualified by the central character, which the man has fashioned for himself. Now the fashioning of character is a moral process. If a man makes no effort at self-control, but follows the impulse of the moment, his character becomes unstable, incoherent, inconsistent, irregular; and in the strict sense of the word, dissolute; for its elements are dissolved, and have no cohesion or consistence of any kind; it is not a unity, but an aggregate of states. If, on the other hand, a man pursues a high ideal, and pursues it with consistency, he learns by degrees to subordinate his inordinate impulses and instincts; to concentrate his attention on one object; to direct his actions to one end; to intensify, and simplify, and unify his life. Thus his metaphysical unity of person is realized in moral unity of character, and he is in harmony with himself. Between these two extremes all human character moves; as a rule neither entirely uncontrolled, nor completely self-determined; the flesh lusting against the spirit, as St. Paul describes it; the charioteer, in Plato's simile, struggling with unequal steeds.

Now of the various and often discordant elements which appear in consciousness, it is only those which have been made objects of will, and so brought into connexion with our moral being, that we strictly consider parts of ourself. No one, for example, feels responsible for the actions of his dreams, because they are not under the control of the will; and it is precisely the same, in our waking moments, with the various sensations and suggestions to which our bodily organism, or the outer world, give rise. They may all be called our own, in the sense of happening to us as distinct from another person. But they are not parts of our self till we have made them so by voluntary acceptance. The bad man is so, not because he is aware of bad impulses, but because he acts upon them; while by the effort of resisting the very same impulses, of which he may be equally aware, the good man becomes good. And thus there is a great deal of truth in the popular use of language which speaks of a good man as a man of character, and of a bad man as a man of no character. For the good man actually has more character to the extent that he has exercised his will, while the bad man is, as we often say, 'not himself,' but the creature of impulse, or the creature of circumstance; the sport and plaything of external forces —less like a person than like a thing. Yet this man all the while is metaphysically speaking a self or self-conscious being, and as such can distinguish himself in thought from the influences which he has lost the power to resist, with consequent feelings which range from self-pity through self-contempt to the deepest remorse. And in the many cases where moral error has gone so far as to unhinge the mind, the interior discord may easily give rise to such a sense of plural personality, as was expressed in the words 'my name is legion, for we are many.' It may be noticed, for instance, that the strongest cases of 'plural personality' quoted by the physiologists are those whose antecedents have been profoundly immoral.

It is perfectly true therefore that our unity of character is a thing of gradual development, wrought out of infinitely complex elements, and varying in degree; and physiological psychology throws much interesting light upon the material conditions of its formation. But the whole process is only possible in virtue of that self-conscious personality, which has no physiological analogue and can only be known from within. This self-conscious personality is, indeed, only known to us in connexion with a bodily organism, and totally disappears at its dissolution. But what then disappears, it must be remembered, is not merely our self-consciousness, but the concrete character which that self-consciousness, in its association with the body, has gradually formed, the moralized or demoralized self. Death is an episode in a moral as well as a physical life, and as such must be morally and therefore teleologically regarded. We are thus led to qualify what the senses perceive in it by what the conscience demands; a continuation of that moral history which in this life is incomplete. And the same moral consciousness which assures us of our personal identity leads us to anticipate its continued existence. Thus the beginning and end of personal identity is metaphysical and moral, and morbid pathology does not affect it. For the fact that its manifestation is obscured by certain diseases is only part of the wider fact that it disappears at death; and if the latter fact does not disconcert our belief, neither need the former. Indeed, both Höffding and Ribot, whom we have quoted above, admit, though it may be thought at the cost of their consistency, that there may be a deeper point of view than the physiological.

‘We note, incidentally, that the theory maintained here, although materialistic in form, can be adapted to any metaphysics. We essay to reduce conscious personality to its *immediate* conditions—the organism. As regards the final conditions of those conditions, we have nothing to say.’ (RIBOT, *Diseases of Personality*, p. 154.)

‘The empirical formula, with which we here end, does not exclude a more comprehensive metaphysical hypothesis. . . . On the contrary, the theory of knowledge leads us to regard the phenomena of consciousness as the most fundamental facts in our experience, since, looked at logically, the subjective point of view is deeper than the objective. From this point of view the most natural conception is that which regards the mental life as the essential, and the corresponding cerebral activity as the form in which it is manifested to sensuous intuition.' (HÖFFDING, *Outlines of Psychology*, ii. 8 d.)

Much valuable sifting of the conception of self will be found in Mr. Bradley's *Appearance and Reality*, where he very truly remarks that 'in personal identity the main point is to fix the meaning of person, and it is chiefly because our ideas as to this are confused that we are unable to come to a further result.' And though the general tendency of his criticism is at first sight destructive, he admits that 'self-sameness exists as a fact, and hence somehow an identical self must be real.' Moreover, it should be noticed that many of the difficulties which he raises, in connexion with this real self, arise from the peculiar canon of reality that he adopts, making it impossible to predicate reality of anything but the Absolute or God—*ens realissimum*; which in a sense, of course, is perfectly true. But if we are content to recognize degrees of reality, we may fairly call the self, as above described, the most real thing that we know, though fully admitting that its reality is and must be derivative and dependent upon God; while of persons, as they exist in the concrete, those who are most moral, and therefore consciously or unconsciously most united to God, are, as we have seen, the most real, and intimately one ; whereas those who are immoral, and to that extent alienated in will from God, are unreal and discordant, to a degree that raises a question in our mind, at times, whether dissoluteness may not end in dissolution ; and the self that has failed to justify its existence cease to exist.

Briefly to resume then : there is—

1. A logical fallacy involved in the attempt to resolve the personal identity of which we are immediately conscious into elements which are only empirically known :—a fallacy which no amount of increase in our empirical knowledge can in the slightest degree affect.

2. Positive metaphysical proof of our personal identity : proof which, though metaphysical, is in no way remote from common sense ; being simply the justification, by philosophical analysis, of what common sense asserts.

3. Moral evidence, which is still more obvious, of the same ; and which consists in (a) our sense of responsibility, (β) our demand of immortality.

And when asked wherein this identity consists, we may be content to reply with Lotze, ' Every soul is what it shows itself to be, unity, whose life is in definite ideas, feeling, and efforts.' In other words, we do not attempt to explain this unity—we merely assert that it exists, and that the efforts of

physiology to account for it are transparently inadequate. There is always a materialistic tendency
abroad in the world, and each new science is pressed
into its service in turn. But, as a matter of fact,
physiological psychology no more makes for materialism than astronomy, or any of the older sciences
which were once thought so to do. Tennyson spoke
as a philosopher, and not merely as a poet, when he
said in words with which we are now familiar: 'You
may tell me that my hand and my foot are only
imaginary symbols of my existence, I could believe
you; but you never, never can convince me that the
I is not an eternal Reality, and that the spiritual is
not the true and real part of me.' (*Life*, ii. p. 90.)

II. FREEWILL

SOME passages from various writers on the subject of freewill, will be found in a note to my lectures on Personality (p. 227): collected partly to show how strong a consensus of opinion there is upon the point, among writers of very various schools, and partly to emphasize the identity of doctrine contained in their different phraseology. But here too, as in the case of self-identity, we are met with objections drawn from physiological psychology; which may justify a few further remarks upon the subject.

In the first place, one must recall the fact that freewill (like personal identity, of which it is a function) is defended on grounds of experience, and denied on grounds of antecedent improbability. As Dr. Johnson once put it when irritated with the argument, 'all theory is against freewill, but all experience is in its favour.' This is important to notice, because it is the exact converse of what is often supposed to be the case; and of what has

always been the case, whenever physical science
has permanently altered popular opinion. For
science is based upon facts of experience, and
when in conflict with popular prejudice, the whole
secret of its success has always lain in its power of
appeal to those facts. But in the present instance
this is not the case. The consciousness of freedom
is a fact of practically universal experience; not of
reported experience in the past, but of present and
past experience alike. While its opponents ground
their opposition, not upon a refutation of the fact,
nor even upon its inconsistency with other facts;
but upon its inconsistency with a theory which they
have drawn from other facts, and can only so draw
by previously ruling the fact in question out of
court. In other words, they beg the question, and
offer presumption instead of proof. And such a
procedure, though due to the influence of scientific
prepossession over certain minds, is radically unscientific and must not be allowed to plead the
authority of science in its behalf.

'Surely the universal conviction of all mankind,
not merely felt but practically adopted in every
action of the whole life of every individual, even by
the philosophers who deny its existence, must be
allowed to count for a great deal in a controversy
of opposing *probabilities*, for it must be clearly
understood that the argument extends to nothing

more than *probability*. The opponents of freedom of
the will do not pretend to prove by the evidence
of facts that this freedom does not exist, but only
that it is highly improbable, because it is, as they
contend, inconsistent with some other accepted
theories.' (Cox, *Mechanism of Man*, i. p. 399.)

Then, after all that has been said upon the
question, there is still a great deal of misconception
as to what is meant by freewill. Every one knows
that it neither means a motiveless nor a limitless
will; and yet on both points there is still a great
deal of confusion.

In the first place it is not motiveless, and to
make this clear, the word self-determination is now
used. But this term, in its turn, has given rise
to misunderstanding, in consequence of its being
appropriated by necessitarians, and utterly distorted
from its original sense. It is universally agreed
that human conduct is determined by motives:
and the only question is whence those motives are
derived. Self-determination means the power of
choosing the motive by which our action shall be
determined, and thus in the last resort, of determining our conduct of our own accord, or as the phrase
says, determining ourselves. Its possibility depends
upon our being self-conscious. For because we are
self-conscious, we can distinguish our 'self' not only
from the external world, but from all the various

thoughts which come into our minds. We can hold
them at arm's length, as it were, and contemplate
them as objects which, though present to our
imagination, are distinct from our self. Now
among these thoughts which come into the mind
are a certain number which arouse our desires, and
therefore appeal to us as motives; urging us to act
or to forbear. But we can treat these precisely
like all other thoughts; we can stand free from
them; we can contemplate them *ab extra*. And
then we can choose from among them which we
will elect to follow. And it is at this point that
we are aware of being free. At the moment
of action we undoubtedly follow what is then
the strongest motive—but it does not become the
strongest till we have made it so by our previous
act of choice: and that act of choice is an act of
pure self-assertion. *I* will make this *my* motive.
I will identify *myself* with this. Self-determination
therefore is simply a more accurately descriptive
name for what is commonly called freewill: and its
accent, so to speak, is upon the 'self.' But various
necessitarians have caught it up and changed its
accent on to the 'determination.' Self-determination, they say, means the fact of being determined
by self, used as a synonym for character; and is
thus only a particular form of determinism; human
conduct being as necessarily determined by character
as material motion by external force. Now this is

exactly what the phrase in question does not mean, and was never meant to mean by those who introduced its use.

Self as synonymous with person, or self-conscious subject, *as such*, is quite distinct from self as synonymous with character, or developed personality, as we have had occasion to point out in the previous note ; and it is in the former sense, and not the latter, that the word is used in the phrase self-determination. It denotes the power that we possess, as self-conscious beings, of selecting our own motives, and so determining our conduct, and through our conduct our character. Of course we have the rudiments of a character, in the shape of disposition and temperament, to start with ; and as this character grows, its influence on our conduct increases. But so far is this influence from being equivalent to self-determination in the proper sense of the term, that we may say with strict accuracy that, in proportion as our character determines us, we are not self-determined ; we do not act as selves, consciously using our power of choice. It is quite true, and a very important truth, that our character, as time goes on, becomes the summary and register of all our previous acts of choice ; and thus expresses our dominant bent, and continues to act automatically, in all the ordinary circumstances of life—just as we write or play music without thinking of the letters or the notes. But though this action is practically automatic, we are conscious of being able, by a sufficient effort, to counteract it ; and it is only because we adopt it by acquiescence, that is by a fresh act of mental self-determination, that we regard it and expect it to be regarded as truly our own.

Self-determination then is only another name for freewill. But it is a more accurate name, for it implies the necessity of motives, as against mere indeterminism, or liberty of indifference ; while it reminds us that those motives are not mere desires, but objects of thought to a self-conscious subject ; who, as such, can distinguish himself from them, and freely decide or decline to make them his own.

The whole process is well described, in somewhat different phraseology, by Professor Case, and the difference of phrase may further emphasize the point :—

'Old-fashioned as it may now appear, the moral commonplace which tells us to govern our passions by our reason, is the real solution of the freedom of the will ; and it is worthy of remark, that everybody remembers this power of the intellect when speaking of virtue, and yet most moralists forget it when they are discussing the will. The real question is, whether the will is independent of the strongest desire, and whether it can choose to follow it or not. The answer is, that the will is free from desire by determining to do what the intellect after deliberation declares to be good, and that it can without reference to the strength of the desire choose to follow it or not,—to follow it, if the intellect declares the object to be good, to reject it, if the intellect declares the object to be evil. . . . The will is neither the child of desire, nor unbegotten, but is the child of the intellect. Though it be true that intellect by itself does not cause action, yet a conception of good in the intellect does cause a volition of good in the will, and is thus through the medium of the will an ultimate cause of action. We control our desires by our will, and our will by our intellect, or by what Butler called "a capacity of reflecting upon actions and characters, and making them an object to our thought." Will then may be defined as the determination to do what the intellect concludes to be good after deliberation. . . . Even if I have not enumerated all the constituents of a free will, I have at least disproved the Necessarian theory, that a man *always* acts from his "desires, aversions, habits, and dispositions, combined with outward circumstances," by proving that he *sometimes* deliberates about the objects of all these motives, and determines to follow them only so far as he judges them to be good. The mere existence of the deliberative intellect is sufficient to disprove Necessarianism.' (CASE, *Realism in Morals*, pp. 16, 19, 24.)

It may be interesting to compare this with the concise language in which St. Thomas expressed the same doctrine six centuries ago :—

'Intellectus movet voluntatem finaliter, quia bonum intellectum est objectum movens voluntatem ut finis.' (*Sum.* 1. 82. 4.)

So far then on the meaning of the phrase self-determination.   The evidence for the fact of it— the fact that we are free to choose between opposing motives—I have attempted briefly to summarize in my lectures on Personality, with further reference in the notes to more authoritative writers, who have treated the subject at greater length.   Briefly the evidence consists in our consciousness at the moment, confirmed by our subsequent approval or disapproval of the choice.   This verdict of consciousness can only be set aside by the arbitrary assertion that it is (and has been from the dawn of history) an illusion or delusion (both terms are used) ; and to support this assertion, two further assertions, of an equally arbitrary nature, are generally made.

1. That we think we could have chosen differently in the past, because on looking back at a later date, and with an altered character, we feel that this altered character *would* have made a different choice.   And on this two remarks may suffice. Firstly, on the necessitarian hypothesis that one choice inevitably leads to the next, the character

could by no conceivable possibility be so altered as to condemn any of its previous decisions, since it would still be moving on the lines which they involved. Secondly, it is not in retrospect, but at the moment of choosing that we are most keenly conscious of our freedom to choose—as when every fibre of our moral being is strained almost to breaking in the agonizing effort of the choice. The subsequent review of a wrong act is, indeed, very far from assuring us that we should have courage to act differently now, as in the case of Sir Walter Scott's Hannah Irwin, quoted by Schopenhauer in his favour: what it does assure us is that we *ought* to have acted differently *then*; and that is precisely *what we remember feeling at the time*, and what convinced us *then*, that we were free.

2. The other assertion is that, as a body which is moved by forces would, if endowed with consciousness, think that it moved of itself, because it followed the strongest force, that is, the force which appealed to it most; so human beings imagine themselves free simply because they are conscious, and therefore aware of acquiescing in the motive that determines them, or wishing what they do. But, as a matter of fact, our consciousness of freedom does not consist in the mere sense of wishing what we do, but in the contemporaneous sense that we could wish or will otherwise *if we chose*. We know very well what it is to be conscious spectators

of our own automatic activities, for it is a familiar experience of everyday life ; but we know, at the same time, that this kind of consciousness differs, *toto caelo*, from our attitude toward acts of will. Yet the statement in question asserts the two things to be identical. It would really seem therefore to be due to confusion—a rather serious confusion—between physical and moral freedom, the freedom of unimpeded, and that of voluntary action. A stone discharged from a catapult, if it suddenly became conscious, would doubtless feel its movement free, in the sense of unimpeded ; but what it emphatically would not feel would be power to change its direction at will. Yet this latter is what we mean by moral freedom ; and the hypothetical analogy in question, therefore, does not touch it, for it only applies to physical or unimpeded, not to moral or voluntary freedom. Hence the supposed delusion of the latter remains precisely where it was before ; except that one more attempt to explain it conspicuously fails.

The same is the case with all attempts to explain the sense of freedom as illusory. They are hypotheses, and from the nature of the case unverifiable hypotheses, invented to justify a foregone conclusion. *Freedom must be an illusion because it ought to be an illusion,* is the sum total of the necessitarian position, when stripped of all disguise. And it ought to be an illusion, because otherwise it would conflict with the reign of law; or more specifically, with the doctrine of the persistence of energy; in accordance with which we are assured, 'a physical movement does not change its direction except under the influence of a physical force,' and there is consequently no room for freewill to intervene.

An illustration will perhaps better enable us to appreciate the case. A financier receives his letters, and, after turning their contents over in his mind, telegraphs his business instructions to various quarters of the world. Or, a woman is seated at the piano, and a friend asks her to play. She thinks over his favourite melodies, or considers his present state of mind, and chooses a particular sonata of Beethoven as the result. Or, again, news is brought to a general of an enemy's movement; he plans how to meet it, and selects a special regiment for the work. Now, in each of these cases, we have physical antecedents, followed by physical consequences. But at a point between the two the human will has intervened, and determined the entire character of the consequences. Other instructions might have been given, other music played, other men sent to risk their lives, and endless differences resulted in the subsequent condition of the external world. Human deliberation has entered as a modifying factor into a series of otherwise physical events, and determined their direction by a conscious act of will. The physical movements do not simply pass into the darkness of the brain, and thence after a while reissue in a definite direction : they report themselves in the full light of consciousness, and are discussed and debated in that light ; and it is exclusively in consequence of what takes place within the sphere of consciousness that they reissue as they do. We have therefore the clearest, the most immediate, the most intimate evidence possible, that our will does, as a fact, direct physical energy.

When, with this in mind, we turn to the statement that 'physical movements do not change their direction except under the influence of a physical force,' we see more clearly to what it amounts. It seems as if it were merely an 'universal affirmative' in physics; but, when used against freewill, it is illegitimately extended into an 'universal negative' in metaphysics ; and 'universal negatives,' as we know, are dangerous to deal with, even in an appropriate sphere. The utmost that the physicist can possibly assert is that *within* the physical region, which is equivalent to saying in the physical region viewed from the physical side, the law in question holds good. But if there is a power outside the physical region, and therefore wholly inappreciable by physical instruments or methods of inquiry, it is obvious that the physicist as such knows neither what it can or cannot do. And that there is such a power, the universal experience of mankind, confirmed by the verdict of critical philosophy, asserts with an emphasis on which, by this time, it is wholly superfluous to enlarge. As Dr. Johnson said, 'we know that we are free, and there's an end of it.'

We have here, therefore, a metaphysical fact of simply incalculable weight, the universal testimony of human consciousness, to what goes on within itself, as against a physical hypothesis, which by its nature can never be universally verified, and least of all in the very region where its verification would be to the point—that is, the living human brain. At the present moment, for instance, we are assured that, 'The relation between nerve-fibres and nerve-cells is very obscure; the physical properties of the ganglia-cells, and consequently the physical origin of the simplest reflex movement, are not yet understood; it is not even quite certain that the ganglia-cells form the connecting-link between the afferent and efferent nerve-fibres. Nor has it been possible to point out the anatomical connexion between the centres of the centripetal and those of the centrifugal nerves in the spinal cord.' (HÖFFDING.)

But let us suppose that all these obscurities have been cleared up by the science of the future, and that the whole mechanism of nervous action can be traced. The verification in question would still be no nearer than before. For even if we could see the continuous action of a living human brain (a considerable concession to the science of the future), we could not tell whether its accompanying consciousness was, or was not, a condition of what we saw. For, as Tyndall characteristically put it, we have not the necessary organ, nor the rudiments of such an organ. There might be no visible breach of continuity, and yet the whole process might be spiritually qualified; much as a living organism qualifies the mechanical properties of its constituent molecules.

It is of course obvious to reply that we cannot logically draw a distinction between the character of movements which are equally physical whether inside or outside the brain. If physical antecedents, without any spiritual coefficient, invariably determine the latter, what right have we to suppose that the former are in different case? When this objection is made by a pure materialist we can only refer him back to those ultimate considerations before which we believe that materialism breaks down. But if it is urged, as is often the case, by those who admit the existence of spirit in the universe; we reply that in that case all physical movement must be conceived to have a spiritual coefficient, as we have argued at length in the text. But if all physical movement has a divine spiritual coefficient, or condition, which is only unobserved because its normal action is uniform, there is nothing illogical, or even improbable, in supposing

that the movements of the brain are specially con-
ditioned or controlled by the spirit of man.   Moreover it must be remembered that, after all, human
personality is, within our experience, unique : to
argue therefore that what does not happen elsewhere is not likely to happen in the human brain
is by no means so logical a proceeding as at first
sight it may seem.   For granting that the human
brain when considered by itself is like any other
'parcel of matter' ; yet in actual fact it only
exists in combination with a unique phenomenon,
a phenomenon which has no parallel within the
range of our experience ; and it is a mere commonplace to say that we cannot infer from what happens
under one set of conditions, what will happen under
another set of conditions, which are not only
different, but as different as we can possibly conceive.   Thus it still remains a case of metaphysical
fact *versus* physical presumption; and the more
the presumption is analyzed the less reasonable is
it found to be.

We may fitly conclude this aspect of the subject
with the following quotation from Lotze, whose
whole treatment of the question should be read :—

'Admitting the incomparability of things physical
and material, it would still be an unfounded prejudice to suppose that only like can act on like, and
a mistake to imagine that the case of an interaction

of soul and body is an exceptional one, and that we
are here to find inexplicable what in any action of
matter upon matter we understand. . . . To our
sensuous imagination, it is true, no interaction but
that of similar elements (similar at least in their
external appearance) presents itself as a connected
image; but it is only our sensuous imagination that
seeks to retain for every case of action the homogeneous character which it fancies it understands
to be an essential condition in this particular case,
and this is just where it deceives itself. . . . The
working of every machine yet known rests on the
fact that certain parts of it are solid, and that these
parts communicate their motions; but how the
elements manage to bind one another into an un-
changing shape, and how they can transmit motions
—and this is what is essential in the process of the
action of matter on matter—remains invisible, and
the similarity of the parts concerned in the action
adds nothing to its intelligibility. When then we
speak of an action taking place between the soul
and material elements, all that we miss is the perception of that external scenery which may make
the influence of matter on matter more familiar to
us, but cannot explain it. We shall never see the
last atom of the nerve impinging on the soul, or
the soul upon it; but equally in the case of two
visible spheres the impact is not the intelligible
cause of the communication of motion; it is nothing

but the form in which we can perceive something happening which we do not comprehend. The mistake is to desire to discover indispensable conditions of all action; and we are only repeating this mistake in another form when we declare the immaterial soul, as devoid of mass, incapable of acting mechanically on a dense material mass, or conceive it as an invulnerable shadow, inaccessible to the attacks of the corporeal world.' (LOTZE, *Metaphysic*, bk. iii. c. 1, p. 436).

But while it is essential to emphasize the existence of freewill, it is almost as important to recognize its practical limitation. For a great deal of the obscurity that surrounds the entire subject is due to the confusion of these two things; the extremely limited nature of our freedom giving superficial plausibility to the denial of its existence. As a matter of fact the power to deviate by a hair's breadth from the chain of physical necessity constitutes freedom, as described above, and renders us in consequence responsible moral agents. And this may be called formal, as distinct from material or practical freedom; meaning that it is a form which has to impress itself on matter; a potentiality ($\delta\acute{u}\nu\alpha\mu\iota s$) which has to be realized, a faculty which has to be used, before we can be called actually and positively free. We are in fact free to become free; free in the first sense to become free in the second sense. And this process of becoming positively free, or realizing our potential freedom, is limited in various ways.

1. We are physically limited by the fact that we cannot create, but can only direct physical energy. This distinction (which Höffding calls a subterfuge) is in fact a very real and important one, for it constitutes the answer to the charge that freewill would introduce confusion into the order of the world. Of course the power to *direct* is as disturbing as the power to *create* energy at will, in the eyes of any psychologist who ever hopes to construct an exact science of the human mind; but this hypothetical science is the only thing that it disturbs. But otherwise, the fact that we can only direct existing energies effectively prevents our disturbing the order of the world; being only the counterpart to Bacon's *Natura non nisi parendo vincitur*. The world is full of forces that every moment are changing their direction, and human action is confessedly one of the factors in this change. But the fact that the action, when regarded from within, is free, does not alter the fact that, when regarded from without, it is like any other physical antecedent, which modifies, but in no way confuses the natural sequence of events. While we are deliberating we are free, but do not alter the material order; but as soon as we begin to act we enter into that order, and thereby become a part of it, and obedient to its

laws. Thus freewill is prevented by its obvious physical limitations from disturbing the order of the world, and what may be called its truly creative force is thereby limited to the sphere of the moral character.

2. But here again it is constitutionally limited, for it cannot create *ex nihilo* ; it can only fashion those rudiments of character which we already possess, in the shape of temperament and disposition, talents, tendencies, and taints. We are free enough to bring a moral or an immoral result out of these elements; but the elements themselves, assisted by the opportunities and circumstances of life, will determine the particular shape of that result, and the consequent individuality of the person. Thus we are constitutionally free to become good or evil, but not to make one hair black or white. We can only realize the individuality with which we were born.

3. But, once more, we are morally limited ; for this very process of realization becomes a further process of limitation in its turn. 'Acts form habits,' said Aristotle long ago, 'because,' adds the modern physiologist, 'nervous energy flows along the line of least resistance,' and habits are, of course, limitations; for the stronger a habit becomes, the less able or likely are we to counteract it. Habits, therefore, grow upon us, good, bad, and indifferent, and 'custom lies upon us with a weight' as life

goes on; and so by degrees our character, or habitual mode of action, is permanently formed. This character, as we have seen above, may still be altered with sufficient effort; but as the effort becomes more difficult, it becomes proportionately improbable, till, in average cases, the necessitarian contention is practically true, that a man's conduct may be predicted from his character, or is, in other words, determined by his past.

Thus our freewill is practically limited in a variety of ways; and it is under cover of these limitations, as noticed above, that its existence can be so plausibly denied. But as a matter of fact neither the physical nor the constitutional limits above mentioned, affect its essence; they merely circumscribe its range. It is only the moral limitation that really affects it, and that is its own creation, for the habits that at last enslave it were at first the objects of its choice; and thus, however much a man's character determines him, he is always and rightly held responsible for the result.

And this leads us to a further point of view. The freewill or power of self-determination which we have hitherto considered, is, as above stated, a potentiality to be realized, a faculty to be used, and its realization is freedom, or the state of being free. But the faculty of freewill is limited on every side. How then can it attain to a state of freedom? Only by making the forces, which limit it, its own; so that they cease to be limitations, and become extensions of itself. Thus a man may assert his formal freewill, by refusing to be controlled, and crossing a railroad in front of a train. He defies his limitations, and immediately loses all freedom in death. While conversely by consenting to be confined within the train, he extends his powers of locomotion to a distance, which they could never otherwise attain, and to that degree enlarges his freedom. By accepting his physical limitation, he enlists its energy on his own behalf, and changes it from a master into a slave. So a criminal asserts his formal freewill to contravene the law of the land, and loses his liberty in prison; while the man who obeys the law of the land, reaps all the fruit of its protection, and thereby obtains a far greater freedom than if the law did not exist. In familiar phrase, we are not free from the law, but by the law; for to obey the law is to identify ourselves with its action, and so to make all its power our own. But to obey law is to surrender our freewill by an act of freewill. Hence, paradoxical as it may sound, freewill (our initial, 'formal,' potential freewill) exists in order to be surrendered, and only by its surrender do we become practically free. At the same time it is the power to make this surrender that constitutes our freedom; it is only because we can choose the law that we can become its agents and not its slaves: and so though our formal freedom is consumed in the using, it is the necessary condition of our being ultimately free. Hence the habits which gradually stereotype our repeated acts of choice, while they limit our freewill, increase our freedom, in proportion as our acts of choice are right. For every region of life has its appropriate laws; and if we disobey them, and by so doing form habits of disobedience, they oppress us with increasing severity till all our liberty is gone; while if we learn habitually to obey them, they extend our power. Healthy habits give us bodily capacity, business habits wealth, studious habits learning, moral habits virtue, spiritual habits piety; and in no case till we have acquired the habits are we really free. Thus the larger the number of rightly chosen habits that we have acquired, or the larger the number of laws that we have learned to obey, the more positively free do we become; since every fresh law that we make our own becomes a fresh instrument for our use; we grow increasingly at home in the world, and its forces are increasingly at our command. While the very fact that our growth in freedom means growth in harmony with the laws of the universe, effectually prevents our freewill from being an element of confusion in the system of things, as some writers and thinkers have supposed that it needs must be.

This leads us to a further and final thought.

The laws of nature are, for theists, synonymous with the will of God. Hence in learning to obey those laws, we are uniting our will to that of God ; and His power becomes our power ; ' Whose service,' in consequence, ' is perfect freedom.'

> ' Our wills are ours, we know not how,
> Our wills are ours to make them Thine[1].'

Or, as Tennyson otherwise expressed it in prose, ' Man's Freewill is but a bird in a cage ; he can stop at the lower perch, or he can mount to a higher. Then that which is and knows will enlarge his cage, give him a higher and a higher perch, and at last break off the top of his cage, and let him out to be one with the Freewill of the Universe.' (LIFE, i. 318.)

' Primum liberum arbitrium, quod homini datum est . . . potuit non peccare, sed potuit et peccare : hoc autem novissimum eo potentius erit, quo peccare non poterit. Verum hoc quoque Dei munere, non suae possibilitate naturae. Aliud est enim, esse Deum ; aliud participem Dei. Deus natura peccare non potest ; particeps vero Dei ab illo accipit, ut peccare non possit . . . ita primum liberum arbitrium posse non peccare, novissimum non posse peccare.' (Aug. *De Civ. Dei*, xxii. 37.)

---

[1] *In Memoriam.* Introd.

www.ingramcontent.com/pod-product-compliance
Lightning Source LLC
Chambersburg PA
CBHW030114030726
47498CB00007B/2379